MW01139215

El Santo

USA TODAY BESTSELLING AUTHOR

M. ROBINSON

This book is a work of fiction. References to real people, events, establishments, organizations, or locations are intended only to provide a sense of authenticity, and are used fictitiously. All other characters, dead or alive, are a figment of the author's imagination, and all incidents and dialogue are drawn from the author's mind's eye and are not to be interpreted as real. Though several people, places, and events portrayed in this book are historically correct, the story is fiction that the author has made up for entertainment purposes only.

Dedication

To Simon (Argie Sokoli)…

I. Love. You.

Boss man: Words cannot describe how much I love you. Thank you for ALWAYS being my best friend. I couldn't do this without you.

Dad: Thank you for always showing me what hard work is and what it can accomplish. For always telling me that I can do anything I put my mind to.

Mom: Thank you for ALWAYS being there for me no matter what. You are my best friend.

Julissa Rios: I love you and I am proud of you. Thank you for being a pain in my ass and for being my sister. I know you are always there for me when I need you.

Ysabelle & Gianna: Love you my babies.

Rebecca Marie: THANK YOU for an AMAZING cover. I wouldn't know what to do without you and your fabulous creativity.

Heather Moss: Thank you for everything that you do!! I wouldn't know what to do without you! You're. The. Best. PA. Ever!! You're NEVER leaving me!! XO

Silla Webb: Thank you so much for your edits and formatting! I love it and you!

Erin Noelle: Thank you for everything you do! And your editing!!

Enrico Ravenna: Thank you for being the perfect muse.

Noemi Rivera: Thank you for your amazing photography.

Michelle Tan: Best beta ever! **Argie Sokoli:** I couldn't do this without you. You're my chosen person. **Tammy McGowan:** I love you!! You have been with me for so long and I couldn't be more grateful for you. **Michele Henderson McMullen:** LOVE LOVE LOVE you!! **Carrie Waltenbaugh:** Thank you so much for your honesty. **Alison Evan-Maxwell:** Thank you for coming in last minute and getting it done like a boss. **Ewelina Rutyna**: I love you! **Mary Jo Toth:** Your boo-boos are always great! Thank you for everything you do in VIP! **Ella Gram:** You're such a sweet and amazing person! Thank you for your kindness. **Tricia Bartley:** Your comments and voice always make me smile! **Kristi Lynn:** Thanks for all your honesty and for joining team M. **Pam Batchelor:** Thanks for all your suggestions. **Susan Pearson:** You are amazing with the honesty! **Patti Correa:** You're amazing! Thank you for everything! **Jennifer Pon:** Thank you for all your feedback and suggestions! You're amazing! **Nicola Spears:** So much love for you!! **Maria Naylet:** I love you to the moon and back. **Deborah E Shipuleski:** Thank you for all your quick honest feedback! **Kaye Blanchard:** Thank you for wanting to join team M! **KR Nadelson:** I love you! **Mel LuvstooRead:** Thank you so much for everything! You helped so much! **Allison East:** Thank you! **Louisa Brandenburger Michelle Chambers, Aidee Cruz, Bernadett Lankovits, Sheila Marie, Leeann Kidson Van Rensburg, Stacy Foster, Betty Lankovits, Emma Louise, Jessica Laws, Lisa Ward, Lily Garcia, Nicole Erard:** Thank you for every laugh, every smile and every single day that you have been my muffin!!

ALL MY VIPS!!!

Jettie Woodruff: You complete me.

To all the bloggers:

A HUGE THANK YOU for all the love and support you have shown me. I have made some amazing friendships with you that I hold dear to my heart. I know that without you I would be nothing!! I cannot THANK YOU enough!! Special thanks to Like A Boss Book Promotions for hosting my tours!

Last but not least.

YOU.

My readers.

THANK YOU!!

Without you…

I would be nothing.

Past

Prologue

Damien

I'm going to tell you a story.

It's dark.

It's brutal.

It's fucking real.

In order to understand my present, who I am, and what I've become…

You need to understand my past.

Evil doesn't always hide in the shadows, in the darkness. Most of the time, it's out in the open, in plain fucking sight. Possessing the man you'd least expect. You see, I never imagined another life until I made one for myself. By that time, I was too far-gone, engulfed in nothing but pitch black darkness. Exactly the way it was meant to be.

No one could touch me.

No one fucked with me.

I. Was. Invincible.

Nothing more…

Nothing less.

When I dreamed of true love—of soul mates, my other half, of her—the cruelty of my life would snap me back into my reality, making it just that, a dream. One that could easily turn into a nightmare.

My worst fucking nightmare.

Every memory, the good, the bad, the in between. All the I love yous, every last I fucking hate you, her heart and soul that I'd broken, shattered and destroyed along the years belonged to me.

Her pleasure.

Her pain.

It was all a part of me, carved so fucking deep into my skin where she would forever be engraved. My story is going to make you fucking hate me as much as she does, but I want you to.

I'm not looking for redemption.

I'm not looking for your forgiveness.

I don't deserve yours like I don't deserve hers.

I'm far from the hero in this story.

I'm closer to the villain.

You will think of me as the villain.

Except, I'm far worse.

I'm the fucking monster.

And, I'm perfectly alright with that.

I dare you to try to love me…

Like she did and probably still does.

Don't say, I didn't warn you.

El SANTO

1
Damien

I gripped my .223 Remington rifle, holding it firmly in my fucking grasp. Feeling the grain of the wood resting securely beneath my fingertips. I was locked and fucking loaded, completely focused on what I had to do next. Tuning out everything around me, waiting for the moment to take my shot. A powerful emotion, one I couldn't begin to describe, immediately washed over me. I felt it deep down to the roots of my core.

I was a man.

A man leading the fucking convoy.

Exactly how our fearless dictator, Emilio Salazar, had done thirty-nine years ago.

"Compañeros, compañeros, queridos, compañeros," he announced, taking his place behind the podium on the stage. Silencing the large, open outdoor stadium where thousands upon thousands of his socialist countrymen were in attendance. Including my father—who was Salazar's right-hand man—and myself.

The crowd stared up at the makeshift stage located in front of the massive yellow concrete building marred with bullet holes and Cuban flags. Taking in every last word that fell from our beloved dictator's lips with wide, eyes, like they always did. Listening intently as he declared this day, July 26th, 1992, the thirty-ninth anniversary of his first monumental attack on the second largest military facility in Santiago de Cuba: the Moncada Barracks. The same exact yellow structure that towered behind us now.

I stood there with pride and honor, wearing military fatigues identical to the ones Salazar wore back on that day. Strategically placing my black combat boots in the same spot he stood when he began his revolutionary movement. I knew it then as much as I had known it in my last eighteen years of life. I wanted everything he had.

The respect.

The power.

The control.

Admiring the leader who almost four decades ago had organized his own military coup alongside a hundred and thirty-five other radicals. Making his presence fucking known.

By declaring war.

Little did the president at the time know that Emilio would devote all his blood, sweat, and tears over the next five and a half years to fulfill his sole promise of a better life. Claiming more cities, taking the lives of the thousands who stood in his way, and growing more powerful until he finally had no choice but to step down to stop the bloodshed.

Fucking pussy.

Emilio may have lost the battle on that day in 1953, but the failure was of no consequence to him or to us. All that mattered was he eventually won the fucking war.

The rest is fucking history.

"I wanted to write this speech to prevent the emotion stemming from this occasion," Salazar professed in Spanish, glancing all around the vast space. Purposely making eye contact with people in the crowd, allowing them to feel like individuals instead of a sea of bodies. He created a profound connection no one could ever comprehend unless they understood that…

To his people.

To his men.

Especially *me*.

Emilio Salazar was God.

I couldn't help but think of the last time I was standing here, only a few short weeks ago. A memory I would take to my grave.

The silence was deafening as the car sped down the vacant road to wherever the hell we were going that day. I just sat in the backseat beside Salazar as the chauffeur drove one of his personal, prestigious vehicles. His security team skillfully outlined the perimeter, driving in front and behind us with a few cars scattered alongside. Even though we were boxed in with armed guards, Pedro—a six-feet-four, two-hundred-and-twenty-pound brick fucking house—still accompanied us in the front seat of our vehicle.

Not to mention, I was fucking strapped too. I'd been carrying a gun since I was un chamaco, a twelve-year-old boy, which was far from fucking normal in Cuba. Salazar had made sure of it. His first order of business after his revolution was to strip every one of their firearms. It was easier to control the dissidents who were still against him, if they couldn't fight back. I was the exception to the rule, given the high position my father held in Salazar's regime. I had no choice but to carry. He was the captain of Emilio's army, which made him just as much of a fucking target as Salazar himself.

My father always said I came into this world kicking and screaming, making my presence fucking known, a force to be reckoned with. A natural-born prodigy ready to fight for a purpose. Although there was a mandatory draft from the ages of seventeen to twenty-eight, which most men dreaded, I busted my ass making sure I graduated a year early. Willingly signing up to serve my country the day I turned of age. Most men only served their required two years, but I had made it clear to my father that the military was my career. Making him one proud son of a bitch.

"Damien," Salazar addressed me, breaking the silence.

"Yes, sir," I replied in Spanish, giving him my full attention.

"Relax, no need for formalities right now. There's a reason I asked you to come with me, and it wasn't for you to kiss my ass."

I breathed out a chuckle, nodding.

"Do you realize I've known you since the day you were born? Your whore of a mother pushed you out of her pussy and abandoned you like you meant nothing. The heartless cunt left you, just like that, and walked out of the hospital hours after giving birth to you. Never looking back. Leaving you to be raised by your father, one of the few men I can truly trust."

I narrowed my eyes at him, trying to figure out where he was going with this. My father didn't speak of my mother very often, and I never asked about her. Salazar was as much of a role model in my life as my father, both honorable men to look up to. I would've rather been raised the way I was, than by the woman everyone claimed was a puta. But I still found myself listening intently as if his words were a piece of the puzzle I never knew needed to be put together.

"The only role a woman needs in a man's life is in the bedroom. Men are what make the world go round. Men like us, we're not followers, we're fucking leaders—we take, we fight, and we kill for our own. We protect with our last breath, if necessary. That's why other people fear Cuba. Fuck Yankee imperialists and their liberal bullshit. I know the right way of life, and so do you. I do this for my people, for my country. I owe it to you, to them, to everybody. America, with their greed and lack of social standards, isn't a way of life. I take from the rich and give to the poor because it's my fucking duty. Damien, one day, one fucking day, you're going to stand where I am, and you're going to show the world that Communism is the only way of life."

As if on cue, the car came to a complete stop in front of the formidable yellow and white building. The Moncada Barracks. His security detail checked the perimeter, opening the doors to our vehicle once it was safe for us to exit. I followed closely behind Salazar, anxiously awaiting what was to come next.

"You're eighteen now, eres un hombre." A fucking man, he said. "The older you get, Damien, the more I see myself reflected in you. It is why I brought you here," he addressed, nodding to the spot where we were standing. "I stood right here thirty-nine years ago with only a vision, a dream of what I could do with my country, and I want YOU to reenact that dream."

I was frozen in place, staring him right in the eyes. Never expecting the next words that came out of his mouth.

He held his head up high and spoke with conviction. "Damien, I want you to be me."

The sound of Salazar's voice brought me back to the present and I shook away my thoughts, not wanting to disrespect my leader.

"Our people have looked forward to this anniversary with love, enthusiasm, joy, and fervor. For me and for those comrades who are still alive, it's a very special experience to meet here with the people of Santiago de Cuba all these years later. To celebrate the action in which our generation opened the path toward the final liberation of our fatherland. None of the predecessors in our people's long struggle for independence, freedom, and justice have had such a privilege." Emilio paused, taking a breath. Allowing his words to once again sink into the depths of our souls.

"It is proper that we pay respectful tribute to those who have shown us the way. To those who from 1868 to today have shown our people the paths of the revolution, who made it possible with the cost of their sacrifice and heroism. Often experiencing only the bitterness of failure and feeling unable to overcome the seemingly infinite, unattainable gap between their efforts and their goals. We needed to go through these primitive years of enriching, unimaginable experiences to acquire the knowledge and maturity in which only the school of the revolution can teach. Everything was like a dream then. Many of our contemporaries, still completely unconvinced that the fate of our nation could and must inevitably change, went as far as to call us dreamers, but I knew better. I led us to this day. I led us to this freedom!" he shouted, raising his right arm up in the air. Making the crowd go wild as Salazar's words drowned out through the speakers, echoing off the concrete walls.

Seeping into the pores of every man, woman, and child in attendance.

I watched and listened, feeling as though he was only talking to me. He entranced me in a way that only Emilio Salazar always had.

I wanted it more.

I wanted it all.

Armed military men raised their rifles up in the air, while I continued to wait. Soon it would be my time to prove that I could fill our leader's shoes. He personally chose me for one reason and one reason alone; he knew I could make him fucking proud. As Salazar continued his speech and spoke about the historical events of that day, his words that stuck out to me the most were of how a true man did not look first on which side he can live better, but on which side his duties lie and that was what shaped the laws of tomorrow.

I was that man.

I was trained to be that solider. That warrior. The one who bled for my fatherland.

Died for my fucking leader.

My duty was to my country.

Serving Emilio Salazar in any way I could. Exactly like my father and the Montero men before him.

"Fatherland or death, we shall win!" Salazar shouted into the microphone for all to relish, but it felt like he was only truly speaking to me. His last words were my cue to spring into action.

My feet moved on their own accord, hauling ass toward the Moncada building, firing off my rifle. Shot after shot rang out with my convoy steady behind me, following my lead. We aimed our rifles toward the barracks, lacing the structure with our bullets, mimicking the shots of 1953 that were still embedded deep into the concrete walls. All I could hear were the sounds of open fire echoing off the building as the crowd continued to go wild. My brothers from the armed forces joined in on the reenactment, setting off their rifles. Only adding to the momentum encased all around me. The adrenaline pumped so fucking hard through my body while my boots pounded into the pavement, one step right after the other. I couldn't get up the stairs and inside the barracks fast enough.

My heart was beating rapidly, I found it almost hard to breathe. My mind raced and my chest heaved with each passing movement, escalating with every gunshot that fell from my rifle. I was a possessed man on a mission, and no one would fucking stop me. To most this was only a reenactment, but to me it was so much more.

It was the first time in my life I ever felt…

Fucking important.

Come hell or high water, no one could ever take that away from me. It was mine. Along with the future of what I'd become.

El Santo…

2
Damien

"You did good, son," my father acknowledged, gripping my shoulder after the parade and festivities had begun. We were standing beside the stage, watching the fireworks go off.

I nodded, trying to hide the smile of satisfaction on my face. My father was a military man, through and through. I could only recall a handful of times I'd ever seen him smile or laugh. He held back his emotions like a shield, saying it was easier for enemies to identify your weaknesses if you wore them on your sleeve. You'd become a target the moment they caught a whiff of feelings, catching yourself a fucking bullet and earning you a place six feet under.

To this day, I didn't know if I would be considered one of his weaknesses or just his son. Physical affection was also a lost concept in my home. When I was a boy, I once asked him why there were never any hugs or love in our home. His response was *"Because I'm not raising a goddamn pussy. I'm raising a man."*

It was the first and last time I ever asked that question.

The only women in my life were the ones who worked for us. I had great respect for all of them, especially our housekeeper, Rosarío. She was the closest thing to a mother that I ever had. When I was younger, she used to be around all the time, but as the years passed, she wasn't needed in our home as often.

It didn't affect our relationship though, I checked in with her every chance I got. Her home always felt more like my own than the one I lived in with my father. It was my favorite part of the week, catching up with her over a cup of coffee and her homemade torticas de moron. Rosarío's husband died at a really young age, and she never remarried. She didn't have any children of her own, but she always told me even though God didn't bless her with her own kids, he gave her me. The affection I lacked from my father, Rosarío made up for tenfold. She'd known me all my life.

As far as girls were concerned, I didn't have time to waste on them. Nor did I give a fuck about the bullshit that came along with dating and pussy. Women were unnecessary complications. A soldier didn't waste time on love or what it entailed.

Nonetheless, I was grateful for and appreciated the life I was given. The world I was born into. There was no other way of life for me. This was all I'd ever known. I had attended the best schools, received the finest education, and knew more about the world than most men my age. I was fluent in five languages, including English, the language of the Yankees.

I never wanted for anything.

My heart was hardened to hide any emotion, like it never existed in my body. I was already conditioned for battle. Taught how to shoot a gun by the time I was five, trained how to fight and kill with my bare hands before I even entered high school. But despite all that, I never witnessed any real acts of violence.

Although it was just my father and I, we had come across hundreds of men in my eighteen years of life. Partially being raised in Salazar's homes, due to the fact my father barely ever left his side. It was the norm to see Emilio Salazar behind closed doors, the power and control he held were things that needed to be admired. When he walked into a room, everyone stopped what they were doing and waited. When he spoke, they listened. When he moved, they watched his every step.

When he…

When he…

When he…

It didn't fucking matter.

All eyes were always on him, no matter what.

The life I lived was one to be envied. Not many men could say the leader of our country was also a second father to them.

"How do you feel?" Salazar questioned in Spanish, walking over to my father and me. "Let me guess, *important*, right?"

I nodded, unable to form words. I wasn't surprised he knew how I felt, he could read everyone like a damn book.

"You are important, Damien. That's why I chose you, and it's time you recognize that. It's your moment to prove yourself to your leader. Do you understand me?"

"Emilio—"

With one look, Salazar rendered my father speechless. For a split-second, I swear I saw fear overtake my dad's eyes, but just as fast as it appeared, it was gone. Quickly replaced with his natural, solemn demeanor. Immediately making me wonder if I had only imagined it.

"With all due respect, Emilio, Damien is merely a—"

"Damien can answer for himself," I crudely interrupted my father, speaking about myself in the third person. Standing tall and stepping out in front of him. Getting right up in his face until my chest touched his. I spoke with conviction. "I don't need you to answer for me, ever! I'm not a child," I affirmed, cocking my head to the side, not holding back. I didn't think twice about putting him in his place, repeating Emilio's words back to him. "Do you understand me?"

Salazar grinned, narrowing his eyes at my father. "He may be your son, Ramón, but let me remind you he answers to me, as do you. Fuck his rank. He proved to me tonight that he's more than ready. He comes with us, and that's an order. Let's go!"

As we made our way to his limo, I was still agitated with my father. I didn't know what bothered me more, the fact that he didn't think I was capable of whatever the fuck Salazar wanted me to take part in. Or the fact that I still sensed he was worried about me. We drove down some dimly lit streets, the tension in the limo was so thick you could cut it with a knife. The silence was almost unbearable. I did my best to ignore it by staring out the tinted windows to pass the time, waiting to reach our final destination. There were three others from the security detail riding along with us, including Pedro. I couldn't help but notice that my father had yet to make eye contact with me. His glare hadn't shifted from his hands clasped out in front of him. Plagued by his thoughts that I knew had nothing to do with my outburst.

I turned my attention back to the road, still not knowing where the hell we were going. Tree after tree whipped by, making it hard to see our path. Blurring into the background. Fading into the distance. I ignored my looming thoughts, focusing on the adrenaline pumping through my veins. Trying my hardest to keep them in check. The last thing I wanted was for them to mistake my anxiousness for fear, or worse, prove that I wasn't ready for this.

When in reality, *this* was all I ever wanted.

The only sounds I could hear were the tires tracking through the unsteady route, my heartbeat, and the thoughts running through my mind. Not one person moved an inch the entire way as the limo continued down its unstable path. It got darker the longer we drove, stirring the mixed concerns in my gut, wondering when the fuck we'd get there. The neighborhoods began to get more rural and run down with each passing minute. Even though I had been packing heat since my twelfth birthday, this could be the first time I would actually have to use my gun. My thoughts incessantly shifted for what felt like the tenth time.

I forced myself to keep my shit together. The eerie quietness wasn't helping my disposition. I felt my nerves creeping up once again, adding to the endless questions I knew I'd never get answers for. The limo's headlights shined off the obscure road until finally all the trees suddenly cleared, and it was then I realized we were in a rancho. We must have been at least an hour away from the city, driving into what was considered el campo—the slums. Now that the full moon wasn't blocked by a bunch of trees, it shined bright against the dark sky, illuminating a vast piece of land. A small, run-down finca-style home that looked like it would collapse on a windy day stood in the middle of the land. The tattered wood siding falling at the seams with paint chips scattered along the hazardous porch. There was a barn in the far back in the same condition, covered by more trees and acres of land.

We were out in the middle of fucking nowhere.

As soon as the driver hit the brakes in front of the house, my father opened his door as if he couldn't get out of the limo fast enough. Salazar and his men weren't far behind him. I instinctively placed my hand on my gun before stepping out into the humid air.

Waiting.

Watching.

Prepared.

Emilio's security team formed a barricade at the front door, my father in the middle, shielding Salazar right behind him. Weapons drawn and aimed at the entrance, anticipating our leader's signal.

The sequence of events that occurred next happened so fucking fast, yet the whole night seemed to play out in slow fucking motion.

Salazar knowingly nodded to my father who didn't have to be told twice. He pulled his guns from his holsters, took a step back, and rammed his foot against the door. The sound of a woman's screams caught my attention first, it was impossible not to hear it. They echoed through the night and the carried cross the acres of open land.

I watched with dark, dilated eyes as Salazar's men, my father included, rushed into the home, not giving anyone inside a chance to run or hide. To seek safety. Nothing.

In that moment, I became fully aware that this was a skilled ambush—one that had been carried out many, many times before tonight. My body voluntarily moved like it was being pulled by a thread, crossing the battered threshold. More ear-piercing chatter rang out, stopping me dead in my tracks. I stood there frozen in place, my feet suddenly glued to the goddamn ground, forgetting for a moment all the years of training I'd had. I quickly shook off the confusion, taking in every last detail like the expert soldier I was.

There were shards of wood from the front door scattered around the foyer. A table overturned in the middle of all the debris. Broken glass from a vase with white ginger mariposa flowers, trampled all over the worn flooring. Family pictures that had fallen from the walls upon impact, casually laying there with smiling faces staring back at me through shattered pieces.

The irony was not lost on me.

My father and his men didn't waver, not even for one fucking second, springing into action. Each of them grabbing ahold of what appeared to be members of a loving family. My father forcefully gripped onto an older man's shoulders, crudely ripping him away from what I assumed was his wife and young daughter. He begged for their lives and they pleaded for his, fighting to get free, reaching their flailing arms out to each other, and praying to God not to hurt him. He must have been in his late sixties, judging by his gray hair and frail appearance. There was no need for the severe assault my father was handing him. The man would have gone willingly, done anything to save his loved one's lives.

"Por favor! Te lo ruego! No las lastimes!" he bellowed, *"Please! I beg you! Don't hurt them!"* in a tone that resonated deep in my core as my father slammed his fist into the side of the man's torso. Making him barrel over in pain.

Pedro held back the young girl who couldn't have been any older than me, while she bellowed, "Papi! Papi! Papi! Por favor! Papi!" The tremor in her voice made me sick to my stomach.

Two of the guards stood watch by the mangled door, closest to me. Not even fazed by the vile scene unfolding in front of them, as if it was nothing out of the ordinary, just another routine night on the job. My eyes shifted to the last guard who had a death grip on the mother, holding her so fucking tight that I thought her arms were going to tear right out of her sockets. Watching her struggle against him, desperately wanting to run to her family. Both of the guards held onto the petite females like they were holding back a couple of two hundred pound men, instead of a couple of fragile women. Manhandling them on purpose, getting off on the fucked-up situation.

"Please! Let them go! It's me you want! Please! Just let them go!" the older man pleaded relentlessly, breathing through the agony of what was happening before him. He tried to fight my father off with all the strength he could muster, clawing, shoving, whipping his body all around. Taking hit after hit my father delivered to the side of his head for each word that fell from his bloody lips. Never once silencing his pleas for their lives.

"NO! Don't hurt him! Please! Don't hurt my husband! We will give you whatever you want! Please don't hurt him! Please! I beg you! Have mercy!" the older woman shrieked while endless tears streamed down her face. One right after the other with no end in sight, mirroring the exact expressions on her teenage daughter's face.

"Te amo, Julio! Te amo con todo mi corazón!" she added, *"I love you, Julio! I love you with all my heart!"* Putting up one hell of a fight.

"Shut the fuck up!" Salazar roared in Spanish. "Shut them the fuck up! NOW! Enough with the theatrics!"

Wasting no time, my father dragged the man to a nearby chair and punched him in the face until he was nearly unconscious. Hanging on by a thread. Causing a trail of blood to ooze from his battered face. His head drooped forward as his body hunched over, going in and out of consciousness. No longer putting up a fight. My father then pulled zip ties from his back pocket, using them to secure the old man's hands behind his back and his ankles to the chair legs.

The two guards, who were still holding the women captive, didn't bother tying them up. Knowing they didn't have to because the women were of no challenge to them. They slapped them around a few times, making their frail bodies even weaker from the force of their blows. Taking hold of their hair, pulling their heads back before placing the barrels of their guns to the sides of their temples. That was all it took to render them speechless, barely being able to hold themselves up any longer.

I swallowed hard when my blank stare found their sadistic expressions. They were showcasing their handy work. Wearing their bloody knuckles proudly.

No remorse.

No guilt.

I couldn't stop myself from looking back at my father, the captain of Emilio Salazar's fucking army, the man who had always taught me that women were different.

They weren't part of the battle.

They weren't casualties.

They weren't prisoners of war.

Our eyes locked across the distance between us, it all made sense now. His stare telling me everything that couldn't be spoken. His concern, his need to speak for me, his shame and remorse currently eating him alive.

They were all fucking lies.

"Damien," Emilio called out, bringing my gaze to him.

It was the first time I ever felt like I was truly looking at him. The real him. Our fearless dictator leaned against the wall, his arms folded over his chest, one leg draped over the other. Not a hair out of place, his military fatigues intact, and a smug expression spread across his fucking face. But that's not what had my attention. It was the fire in his eyes, burning into my soul.

He was getting off on this as much as his men were.

The power.

The control.

The fight he brought into this family's home.

"I know what you're thinking," he acknowledged, nodding to me. "Things aren't always the way they appear. I can see the judgment in your eyes, it's radiating off your body. You dare judge me, your leader who has done nothing but turn you into a man? I made our country what it is today, and you still stand there and question me? Are you questioning your loyalty to me because of a couple of whores and an old fuck? Eh?" He pushed off the wall, placing his hands into the pockets of his pants. Slowly walking over to where my father stood with the older man who was still struggling to stay alert.

"I didn't say a word," I simply stated, watching his every move.

"You didn't have to. You see, Damien, I was once like you."

I blinked, taking in his words, still completely aware of my surroundings. How the guards kept fucking with the women, running their guns down their breasts, stomach, and thighs. Making their torn, flimsy nightgowns stick to their sweaty skin. Pressing their cocks into their asses, purposely making their terrified bodies sway against their dicks. The only sounds that could be heard were their low, subtle whimpers, knowing they probably would not make it out of here alive. The men who were standing guard by the doors just waiting for their fucking turns.

I played my part, acting as if I didn't notice the invasive acts. Giving the monster standing in front of me exactly what he craved.

Respect.

"I wanted to protect my country, I wanted freedom for all my people, I wanted a life where everyone was equal. I—"

"Everyone but you," I interrupted, standing taller, not backing down.

He grinned, peering up and down at me. "And you. What? You think you're not treated different? Held to higher standards? Given privileges most would die for? Oh, come on, Damien… look in the goddamn mirror. You're just fucking like me. Always have been and always will be. You should be thanking me, not doubting me. The man who has given you everything!" he seethed, making the women yelp in response. "There isn't anything running through your little mind that couldn't be more wrong. You see this man?" He roughly grabbed ahold of the father's hair, jerking it back so I could see his mangled face. "This man is a fucking traitor!"

"What did he do? Not pay his fucking taxes because he had to feed his family?!" I spewed the truth, the one I'd been hiding from myself my entire life.

Emilio cocked his head to the side, once again eyeing me up and down with a look I'd never seen before. "He was working with the enemy to bring me down. He and a bunch of other traitors were having meetings in this house! Organizing my demise to bring down everything I've worked for my whole life! And do you know what we do to traitors?" He paused, shoving the man away, causing his chair to stagger.

An eerie silence filled the room as he walked toward the women, beaming from ear to ear. Enjoying the effect he evoked on the helpless women. Both tried to weakly back away from him, only sinking further into the guards' dominant hold. Salazar didn't hesitate, pulling the teenage girl away from his henchmen.

"NO!" the mother shrieked an ear-piercing scream that would forever haunt me.

That night and his words would change who I was, and everything I believed in for the rest of my life.

It all started with…

Four simple words.

"We make them pay."

3

Damien

The girl immediately started screaming and thrashing around in Emilio's arms. Her long brown hair stuck to the sides of her swollen cheeks. Endless tears streamed down her pretty, bruised face as she fought the monster who invaded her home in the middle of the night. Salazar didn't pay her any mind, amused by the turn of events. I didn't think twice about it, pulling out my gun and aiming it point blank to the middle of her father's forehead. Never breaking my intense stare with Salazar.

I narrowed my eyes at him, speaking with execution, "I'll pull the fucking trigger myself as soon as you let the women leave safely."

Emilio smiled, big and wide. Looking down at the girl who was now glaring at me with a new sense of hope in her dark brown eyes.

"Don't try to be the fucking hero in this story, Damien. There's only one thing you need to learn from tonight. The only way to make a man pay for his sins… is always through the ones he loves the most."

Her mother started breaking down, screaming and trying to claw her way free. Doing everything in her power to save her daughter. While the father came to, begging for their lives from his chair. Pleading with everything inside of him to let his girls go.

I didn't waver, pointing my gun to the man's shoulder and pulling the trigger.

"NOOOOOO!" the women screamed in unison, fighting with every last ounce of strength they had to go to him.

"Next bullet is through his heart!" I yelled, needing to get my point across. "Now let them go!"

"Stand the fuck down, soldier!" Salazar ordered, knowing I had no choice but to listen.

For the first time in my life, I fought an internal battle between what was right and wrong. Lowering my gun, trying like hell not to let the chaos cloud my judgement. Salazar was over to me in three strides with the daughter in tow, tearing the gun out of my hands. Dragging her to her feet in front of him, setting the cool metal on the side of her head instead. He placed her securely in between us, a few feet away from me. The girl's eyes spoke volumes, intensifying with each second that passed like a ticking time bomb.

Fear.

Pain.

Death.

"It's time you man the fuck up and prove to me who you stand by. Where your duties lie because fatherland or death, we shall win!" With that, he shoved her as hard as he could in my direction, causing her to lose her footing.

She whimpered as I caught her in my arms mid-fall. Supporting her small frame against my chest. Our faces inches apart as she instinctively tried to fight me off. Not that I could blame her, I was just another villain in her eyes.

"Control her! Show her what we do to fucking traitors! Do you understand me?" Emilio roared, making her struggle against me even harder.

I couldn't do it, I took every blow she delivered. Allowed her to feel any solace I could provide, even if it was only for a few seconds. It was the least I could do. She began to hit me harder and harder when she realized I wasn't stopping her, I wasn't fighting back. I was letting her have her moment.

"Now is your time to truly prove your loyalty to me! Show her who she serves!"

When I didn't do what he wanted, Salazar crudely tore her away from me by her hair with revulsion in his eyes. Her hands instantly went to her head where he had ahold of her, wincing in pain. Clawing at his fingers as he hauled her over toward the guards by the door. Her legs flailed behind her, trying to gain control to stand up steadily, but failing miserably.

Her father started whipping around, desperately trying to escape from the chair—harder, faster, almost knocking it over. The blood gushing from the bullet hole in his shoulder not stopping him. While her mother did the same with the fucking guard.

It was then I locked eyes with my father, his stare begging me to forgive him. To have mercy on him too.

"This is what we do to men who betray us, Julio," Emilio rasped the father's name in a menacing tone that made my body shudder. Nodding to one of the guards on watch at the door, handing her off to him instead. As if he didn't want to get his hands dirty from the filth, like she was just a piece of trash.

"Do your best, *puta*. No one can fucking hear you out here," the guard baited, tugging her over to the small beat-up couch in the living area. "I love it when they scream," he added.

"No!" she shouted, pathetically thrashing around her entire body, kicking, and hollering at the top of her lungs as she repeated, "Please!" over and over again. Hoping at any second she would wake up from this horrid nightmare. God would save her from this Hell. "No! No! No!" she continued to yell out to no avail, making them all laugh and me fucking sick.

Emilio nodded to my father, silently ordering him to shut the old man up. He did, forcefully slamming the handle of his gun down onto the back of his neck. Knocking him to the floor with the chair. The guard who held the mother covered her mouth to muffle her screams, but she didn't stop fighting him until he punched her in the stomach. Sending her to her knees in pain.

His henchmen ripped off the girl's panties, tossing them to the floor. Her nightgown was already torn, leaving her exposed and practically naked. He pushed her over the arm of the sofa, shoving her head into the cushion, and holding her down. Making her ass stick out in the air.

"That's enough!" I growled, my chest rising and descending. I couldn't watch this any longer.

"What, Damien? She's a beautiful girl, isn't she? Don't you want your first taste of pussy? She's a whore just like your mother," Emilio snarled.

"Fuck you!" I seethed, my hands balling into fists at my sides.

Before I got the last word out, he cold-cocked me with the butt of my gun. My head whooshed to the side from the forceful impact of his blow. It was the first time Salazar had ever hit me.

"I've given you everything, boy! Are you going to let this traitor take away all you believe in?! Maybe I should let him bend you over and fuck you instead!" he threatened, shaking his head. "No, that's not how this is going to go down. You show this motherfucker that we do not and will not allow traitors in our country! He took from us, so now the time has come to take from him! You take his daughter! You take her right in front of him and make him watch. Pay for his sins! No one betrays us!"

I didn't move, spitting a mouthful of blood onto the floor near my feet, as the young girl turned her head away from the couch cushion. Staring into my eyes, pleading with me to save her.

Save them.

"Be a fucking man! She's nothing! Take control! I know it's in you, just like it's in me and your father!" Not allowing me the chance to reply, he simply raised the gun and aimed it in the center of my forehead. Snarling, he added, "It's why I chose you! Now make me fucking proud!"

I didn't falter, shouting, "Then pull the fucking trigger!"

He jerked back, completely caught off guard with my reply. If tonight proved anything to him, it was the fact that I didn't want anything to happen to the women, and the son of a bitch used it against me. He instantly moved my gun, aiming it at the mother and pulled the trigger.

"NO!" I yelled out, about to run to her aid as she suffered in agony, but Pedro grabbed ahold of me. Locking my frame in place.

"Next bullet is through her heart," Emilio stated, throwing my words back at me. "Do it or she dies! You want to be responsible for taking this girl's mother away? What kind of *monster* are you?" he mocked in a condescending tone, smiling deviously.

My eyes found the girl's staring back at me for a split-second before she clenched them shut, like it hurt her to look at me. Turning her face away in defeat. Pedro started walking forward, taking me with him willingly. There was no use to resist, Emilio had me right where he wanted me.

Prisoner.

Once we were close enough, he forcefully pushed me into the girl. I caught myself on the back of the couch before my weight fell forward, crushing her frame. Her body shook so fucking hard against my chest, sobbing to herself. All the fight she had before was gone, and I resisted the urge to fight for her. We both knew damn well if I did, it would cost her mother her life. And probably ours too.

"Shhh..." I whispered close enough to her ear where no one could hear. Her mom's wails from the gunshot filled the room, making it easier to be discrete. I tried to steady her breathing, calm her in any way I could. "Shhh..." I repeated a few times until I felt her start to settle down. She turned her head slightly, our eyes barred into each other's.

With trembling lips, she murmured, "I'm a virgin."

And with a sorrowful glare, I responded, "So am I."

For just that moment in time, we stared at one another, both of us trying to crawl into that empty space inside of our minds.

To hide.

To seek refuge within ourselves was the only way we were going to survive this. Drown out the turmoil erupting all around us, muffling the screams with our plaguing thoughts. The pleas disappearing into the distance while we visibly struggled with our conflicting emotions.

"Please, God," she prayed, for I don't know what.

After tonight, I was convinced there was no God.

At least not…

For me.

"Como te llamas?" I tenderly asked, *"What's your name?"*

"Teresa," she breathed out, gazing deep into my eyes, intently searching for something behind my stare.

"Perdóname, yo trataré de no herirté," I sincerely voiced, *"I'm so sorry, I'll try not to hurt you."* Mirroring her intense gaze, I swept a strand of hair out of her face with the back of my hand. Allowing my fingers to linger on her soft, velvety skin.

She quickly pulled away from my embrace, narrowing her eyes at me. "Do your worst, *boy*. He's right. You're just like him. The only difference is you're a monster who doesn't know it yet. He knows it and has accepted it, and after tonight, you will too. Just do it. Stop pretending to be something you're not."

I jerked back like she had hit me, shattering from the reality of her words. The remnants of the man I thought I was would be dead after tonight. There would be nothing left of me. I had to turn off my humanity to push through this or we wouldn't make it out alive. What happened next was like I was having an out-of-body experience.

I was there… but I wasn't.

I vaguely heard Salazar taunting, "You pussy! You can't even get hard! Do it now! I'm losing my fucking patience!"

Another bullet flew toward the mother, barely missing her head that time.

More screams.

More laughter.

More sins I would have to pay for.

I knew Teresa could feel me everywhere, and I was barely even touching her, revolted by what I was doing. With what I had to do. I could sense a throbbing burn radiate throughout her entire body from the sudden loss of breath. The wind being knocked out of her with my weight resting on her back.

I sucked in air that wasn't available for the taking. Bile rose in my throat. The control, the power, the feel of her tight pussy wrapped around my cock, slowly crept in, finding its way inside of me.

Fucking with my mind.

I tried to drown it out, willing myself not to feel anything but the vicious act I was delivering.

Suddenly realizing tears were streaming down my face. My lips quivered, my teeth chattered, and my vision turned black, blinking away the white spots. When she moved her hips, I instinctively gripped onto them hard, causing her to whimper from the unexpected pain.

"Don't fucking move," I gritted through a clenched jaw, unable to control the sensations her pussy stimulated, needing to control the rhythm of our sinful act. Hating myself more for it. It was too much for me to take, awakening a beast, a dark side of me that I never knew existed.

Imprisoning my body, mind, and soul.

I could feel her virtue, her goddamn innocence on my cock; it only added to the conflicting emotions stirring in my mind. With each thrust, I felt the demons that would eternally haunt me. Torment me until the day I died, until I took my last breath. I didn't walk through the valley of the shadow of death that night…

I would now fucking live there.

Permanently residing inside of me.

Where I would never make it out alive.

It was all too much—the voices, the commands, the fucking sensations. My hips started moving on their own accord, like I was a possessed goddamn man.

The sinner taking over while the saint sat silently by his side.

My fingers tightened, digging my nails into her flesh, picking up my speed. Thrusting into her harder, faster, stronger. My vision tunneled, and I swear I heard her moan over the madness living inside and all around me. Only tempting the fiend further, causing my head to fall forward onto her neck. I tightly shut my eyes. Seeing flashes of Teresa's crying face, blood…

So much fucking blood.

I shook off the images as quickly as they approached, the saint defeating the sinner, pulling me back into the light. Finally taking possession of my actions. Control of my life. I had to put an end to this, unable to keep dragging another life down to Hell along with mine.

Right when I was about to finish…

I heard the girl's father shout, "Amira! NO! Run!"

I instinctively turned to the guard on my right, grabbing the gun from his holster, and pointing it in the direction of the shadowy figure beside me. Coming face to face with a little girl whose wide brown eyes would now be seared into the darkness of my life.

Knowing she saw *everything.*

I glanced around the room, needing to see it through her eyes. Her mother lying there, bleeding out, still trying to form screams that came out as whispers. Her father tied to a chair, franticly begging her to run. Her sister bent over a couch, crying uncontrollably with me still inside of her.

With the gun still firmly in my grip, pointing to her head, aimed to kill her.

I immediately lowered my weapon, feeling like the monster I knew I was. I adjusted my pants, looking up just in time to see Salazar raise my gun out in front of him.

"Nooooo!" I shouted, running toward him.

He didn't falter. "Deal is off!" Opening fire around the room, killing Teresa first. Wanting her parents to see her die, no matter what.

I caught her before she fell to the floor with a hard thud, tugging me with her. Cradling her lifeless body in my arms, I applied pressure to the bullet wound in her chest. "What the fuck did you do?" I franticly asked, staring at the lifeless face of Teresa, the girl I had only just met.

Her father's agony brought my attention back to Salazar. I dreadfully watched as he murdered her mother next, making the man witness his family being slaughtered right before his eyes.

"Fatherland or death, we shall win," were the last words he heard before Salazar killed him point blank. Putting an end to the "theatrics" as he called them.

I once again sucked in air that wasn't available for the taking, each shot resonated deep into my core. My chest heaved with every breath, suffocating in the massacre all around me. Drowning in the devastation of every life brutally ripped out of this world. I peered down at the girl in my arms again, her innocent blood on my hands.

Along with her family's.

Swallowing hard, I glared up at Emilio with nothing but hatred and remorse in my eyes. "We had a deal," I shook out, pitifully trying to gather my words.

My emotions.

The soldier was long gone.

Disappeared into the night as if he never existed to begin with.

Salazar chuckled, "Motherfucker, you didn't even come," he sadistically spewed. Nodding to the little girl who stood there paralyzed with her doll tight in her grasp. As if she was holding onto her most prized possession. All the color drained out of her body, going into shock. Her traumatized eyes connected with mine, instantly searching for answers to questions I would never be able to give her.

A single tear escaped, slowly falling down the side of her face, off her chin, and onto the floor. Rippling in her sister's blood. I swear I could fucking taste…

Her pain.

Her loss.

Her future forever changed.

"She's yours now," Emilio added, throwing my gun back at me. Nodding to the little girl, he spoke with conviction. "She can be your daily reminder of the family you took away from her and what happens when you betray me."

It was only then that I realized I lost more than my life that night.

I lost my fucking soul.

All in the name of communism. And a man more evil than the Devil himself.

4
Amira

“Amira! NO! Run!” Papi screamed, but I could barely hear him over the commotion.

I didn’t want him to be mad at me.

I didn’t want to be a bad little girl.

I didn’t want to let my family down.

Hearing the yelling and the loud gunshots. Watching the pain and agony they were going through.

It hurt all over my body.

I felt it on every last inch of my skin.

I would hear their screams every time I shut my eyes. See their bloody faces every second of the day. Reliving each plea, each bullet, and each mark on their battered bodies.

I felt it all.

In my mind, body, and soul.

I hid for what felt like hours, witnessing it all through the tiny hole in the kitchen cabinet. It had always been my favorite hiding spot while playing hide-and-go-seek with Teresa. No one ever found me when I hid in there. I held my breath to keep from making a sound. Peering out into the living room where a bunch of monsters were torturing my family. The nasty men my father told me to hide from weeks before. I wanted to close my eyes like I was watching something scary, and it would make it go away. As if it was only a bad dream that I would soon wake up from. But every time my eyes hid in the darkness, it only made my thoughts worse. Not knowing what was going to happen next. Making it harder to control my emotions and fear. I had to watch no matter what. It was the only way I would be able to keep my promise to Papi.

My terrified stare flew to the man walking into the living room. The monster, holding my family hostage, Damien. I couldn't take my eyes off the tall man who was standing a few feet away from my secret spot. Still hidden behind the thin wood cabinet door. He was wearing military fatigues like the men who would come collect our food every month. I noticed his demeanor instantly. I could see something different in his honey-colored glare. The way he was looking at my family, how his hands slightly twitched with his sincere expression. The way he stood by the door, not moving an inch. Watching everything play out in front of him, exactly how I was.

He wasn't like them.

They were monsters in his eyes too.

I silently prayed he was going to be my family's savior. He'd become the hero in this nightmare. The longer I watched, the more I realized he was just as much of a victim as my whole family was. He didn't want to do those horrible things.

He was fighting for their lives, while I hid fighting for mine.

More screams.

More gunshots.

More…

More…

More…

"Next bullet is through her heart. Do it or she dies! You want to be responsible for taking this girl's mother away from her? What kind of monster are you?"

I wanted to scream, *"He's not a monster, you are!"* But instead, I hid my face into my doll Yuly's body. It was too hard to keep watching their pain. My broken heart was now in my throat with bile rising, but I swallowed it back down. Covering my ears with my hands, trying to drown out Mami's wails and the monster's voice. Remembering the last time I was happy with Papi.

"Amira, I have a present for you," Papi revealed in Spanish, touching the end of my nose with his index finger. A gesture he'd been doing all my life. He would tease that my nose would grow like Pinocchio's if I told lies. It was his way of making sure he kept me honest.

My father worked day in and day out in El Campo, the city, and anywhere else he could get goods in exchange for his labor. Whatever that meant.

I hadn't seen him in a few days which made me really sad. It felt like every time he left to go into the city to work, the longer it took him to return. I hated when Papi left, things weren't the same without him.

Mami and Teresa missed him, too, but not like I did. Mami would try to cheer me up every time he left by letting me play with the baby chickens out in the barn. Or she'd let me run free in the field and pick my favorite flowers, mariposas, for Papi. A delicate white flower with petals that formed the shape of a butterfly. When he was home, I'd flap my arms up and down like I was flying, and twirl all around him, making him laugh and smile.

Those were the best days.

Papi knew I was unhappy when he left us, so he'd always try to bring me back a gift, to make up for his absence. Knowing it was rare for us to receive any presents unless it was our birthday or a holiday. No matter how big or small it was, I cherished everything he ever gave me because it came from his good heart.

The same heart I had in my body. Papi was my hero, and I loved him very much.

With wide eyes, I watched as he stood up and showed me what he was hiding behind his back this whole time.

"Papi," I gasped. "You got me one!" Jumping up and down, unable to control the excitement running through my body.

He mischievously grinned, handing the doll over to me. I never had a baby doll before. I'd been asking for one since Claudia brought hers to school two years ago. Saying her papi found it on the bus. I secretly wished mine would find one on the bus too. He knew it was all I ever wanted.

Toys were hard to come by. I hardly ever got any since all of Cuba's goods came from the Soviet Union, who didn't have much to part with. Plus, the United States didn't want to help us anymore. At least that's what I overheard Papi's friends say when they came over with all their maps and papers. Spending hours upon hours talking about political imprisonment and corruption. Three words I learned the meanings of from the only dictionary we had at school the next day.

When I asked Papi about it a few days later, he told me not to be upset with America. They were only doing what they could to make Emilio Salazar surrender and step down. He made me promise to never hold hatred for anyone in my heart; it only led to bad things. To love everyone the same, especially those who needed it the most. Telling me that sometimes there were people in our world who were just lost souls and needed our help to find their way.

I smiled big and wide, instantly hugging the doll as hard as I could. Showing her how much I loved her. Bringing the baby up to my face when I was done to take a good look at her. Claudia's doll had a scratch on her face and was missing shoes and the ribbons out of her hair. Mine was perfect, her long, dark brown hair and brown eyes looked exactly like mine. She was wearing a white dress that flowed down to her feet, with black shiny shoes. There wasn't a mark on her, she looked brand new. I immediately wondered where Papi got her from, but I'd never ask.

I couldn't hold in my happiness, emphasizing, "Oh, Papi! I love her! I love her so much!" I cheered, hugging her close to my heart again, needing to feel she was really there.

She was really mine.

Before I gave it another thought, I tackled Papi's legs. Squeezing them in a big, tight hug. Hoping he could feel all the love and appreciation pouring through my embrace.

"Thank you! She will never leave my side! Now I don't have to be sad when you leave, Papi. You'll always be with me through her," I let out, holding back my tears. I was so overwhelmed. I couldn't believe he got me a baby doll.

He didn't waver, grabbing ahold of my arms and crouching down to my level. Placing me in front of him so I could see his face. He had tears in his eyes, wearing an expression I'd never seen before.

My heart dropped. "Papi—"

"Amira..." He paused as if he was trying to gather the strength to tell me something. This didn't feel right, my papi was the strongest person I knew, he never cried.

I pulled my arm away from his grasp, placing my hand on the side of his face. Caressing his cheek, trying to give him the courage he needed to keep going.

It worked. He coaxed, "I need you to promise me something."

I fervently nodded, wanting to do anything to wipe the look off his face. It was hurting my heart.

"I need you to listen to what I say. I need you to be my good little girl and listen to me, okay?"

"Papi, you're scar—"

"If any nasty, mean men ever come into this house, Amira, and you hear screaming and bad things..." He hesitated again, making my heart beat faster. His words not coming out as fast as the thoughts running through his mind. "If you hear anything out of the

ordinary, Mamita, and you feel scared... I need you to promise me you will hide."

I stepped toward him. "Papi —"

He stopped me dead in my tracks, holding me steady in place like he needed to look into my eyes. "Do you understand me, Amira?"

Why would I hide if I was scared? I never had to do that before. He always chased away the monsters in my bad dreams. Maybe he needed me to chase away his monsters too?

"Do you understand me? You hide," he reaffirmed, as if he knew what I was thinking.

I nodded again, unable to say the words.

"Amira, promise me... You swear to me that you will hide from the bad men. No matter what, you hide. And you hide until you don't hear another word or scream," he demanded, even though his mouth was trembling. His eyes holding so much sadness.

"But, Papi, what if—"

"Nothing! You hide!" he ordered in a harsh tone, making me jump. He never yelled at me before. "No matter what you hear or how much it hurts you to hear it... you hide, Mamita. Please... promise me you'll hide," he begged, his voice breaking.

I bit my lip, holding back my tears. I didn't want him to see me cry. He was already sad enough. I always listened to what my papi said because I was his good little girl. I didn't want to disappoint or let him down.

I stood tall, wanting to be his brave Amira. Needing to be strong for the both of us.

"I promise, Papi. I promise I will hide. I'll hide and not come out until it's safe, okay? I won't come out until you tell me it's safe, okay? You'll tell me to come out, right, Papi? You promise you'll come get me? After the monsters are gone?" I asked with quivering lips, my voice faltering.

My heart shattering.

With tears falling from his eyes, he simply stated, "I love you, my tiny shadow. No matter what, I will always be with you." He placed one hand over my heart and the other on my doll. "In here."

It wasn't until that night that I realized… he never promised he'd come get me. I didn't know how long I stayed in the shadows of the cubby, but it felt like forever. When I took my hands away from my ears, all I could hear were the men laughing. I moved Yuly away from my face, peeking through the tiny hole in the cabinet again. All I saw now was Damien's back. He was behind Teresa, who was bent over on the couch cushion in front of her. He was moving his hips as if they were playing some sort of dancing game.

When Damien ordered, *"Don't fucking move,"* to Teresa, I came out of hiding.

I made my way out of the safety of the small space as quietly as I could, needing to go get help. Clutching Yuly close to my chest, hoping she would cover the sounds of my rapidly beating heart. Thinking maybe they could hear it. I breathed a sigh of relief when I made it out of the kitchen without being seen. I softly walked down the hallway, where they couldn't see me and I couldn't see them. Stopping when I heard Teresa make a noise that sounded like a cry of pain but comfort too.

I heard Papi scream my name, from the chair he was tied to, before I even realized what I had done. It was too late to turn back. The gun in Damien's hand was now pointed directly at me. I'd never seen a gun up close. I instinctively hugged Yuly harder.

Seconds turned into minutes and minutes seemed like hours as I stood there, anticipating the worst.

The next few moments of my life happened in slow motion. Mania erupted in our once loving home, but I didn't hear a word that came out of anyone's mouth. The sounds of my heart beating its way out of my chest took over my senses. My ears were ringing from the palpitations, and my vision tunneled. Papi's words from a few weeks ago, mixed with the screams of my name, played like a broken record in my subconscious.

"Amira, promise me... You swear to me that you will hide. No matter what, you hide. And you hide until you don't hear another word or scream."

I could feel my body shutting down and my mind going into a dark place inside of me, where no one could hurt me. Shot after shot rang out, causing my body to jerk with each and every one of them. Bullet casings started falling to the floor followed by their bodies. I felt like I was suffocating from the emotions that I felt in a split second.

Regret.

Grief.

Anger.

Hope.

All of them hitting me at once, as if my papi, mami, and sister's souls were holding onto mine for dear life. I didn't think it was possible to feel so much and not physically die right along with them.

I was.

I had.

There was this imaginary line that was pulling deep within my bones. I felt it from my head down to my toes. It was flashes of the life that wasn't mine anymore. My past taunting me and comforting me simultaneously.

My vision suddenly cleared when I faintly heard, *"She's yours now. She can be your daily reminder of the family you took away from her, and what happens when you betray me."*

All the night's memories came tumbling down, burying me in the rubble of their blood. I couldn't breathe, staring into the eyes of the man I thought was going to save us all. I was terrified that if I looked away, he would disappear. A huge part of me didn't want him to leave. I knew if he did, I'd be alone with only my thoughts and feelings. The physical need to die with them.

The nightmares I would never survive.

The longer I stared into his eyes, the louder his internal thoughts got. Repeating… *"I'm sorry, I'm sorry. I'm sorry,"* over and over again with no end in sight.

This wasn't a nightmare.

This was my reality now.

The monster in the night walked out of my home. Crossing the mangled threshold they so harshly brought down, with two of his men by his side. The home he destroyed with nothing but corruption, violence, and murder. Never once looking back at the reality that was now my life.

I was the first to break Damien's intense stare, shifting my eyes to my sister, my father, and my mother…

They weren't smiling.

They weren't laughing.

They weren't moving.

There was no soul, no life, no love.

Nothing.

They were all dead.

The string that connected me to the man named Damien snapped…

And I ran.

I ran on pure impulse toward my father, running as fast as my legs would allow me to go. Falling to my knees in all the blood pouring out of his unrecognizable face and body.

"Papi! You gotta wake up!" I coaxed, placing my trembling hand everywhere not knowing where to stop the bleeding. "Please… Papi… you gotta help me wake up Mami and Teresa… I can't do this alone… so wake up now, okay?" I threw my arms around his body, shielding him from bleeding out with Yuly in between us. Closing my eyes as tight as I could. I cried over his body, shaking him so hard to wake up. "Remember, you promised you were going to take me to the city? We were going to see the world? Remember, Papi? You promised…"

He wasn't moving.

He wasn't waking up.

There was nothing I could do.

"I'm sorry, Papi! I'm sorry, I didn't stay hidden. Please… don't be mad at me… I'm still your good girl, right?"

"He's fucking dead, you stupid girl. Your family's dead. How's it feel to be a fucking orphan?" one of the guards hollered from across the room.

I slowly sat up and stood, rooted in my spot, looking at the lifeless bodies. Taking in his words. There was so much blood all over me and Yuly, I couldn't even see my skin. I bowed my head, so much guilt and regret hitting me harder than anything I'd ever experienced before.

Maybe if I would've stayed hidden they would still be alive?

Fresh tears leaked from my eyes, and it took everything in me not to continue to beg for his forgiveness.

"I asked you a question," the man spewed, making me gaze up at him through the slits of my swollen eyes.

"I hate you," I whispered so low he couldn't hear.

"What was that? I can't hear you over the sound of your pathetic whimpers."

"I said," I stood taller with Yuly, my hand clenching into a fist, "I HATE YOU!" I seethed, charging the two men beside Damien in the room. Hitting, punching, pushing them as hard as I could. Making them laugh at me. Only fueling my hatred more.

I fought with every ounce of strength I had left inside my hollow shell, still holding onto Yuly. Needing her comfort to keep going. I shoved, slapped, and hit the murderers, wanting to hurt them. Pounded my fist into their rock-hard chests, not paying any mind to the throbbing pain running through my hand. It was nothing compared to the knife in my heart. I just wanted them to die too. I kneed the biggest man in between his legs so hard that I fell back on the broken glass, wincing instantly from the pain.

His hand instinctively went up in the air about to slap me across my face, but a strong arm wrapped around my stomach, yanking me back. Lifting me off the floor, just missing the large man's hand as it whooshed by my face. As soon as my back collided with someone's solid chest, I turned around in their arms and fought.

"No! No! No!" I shrieked, roughly trying to fight him off. Shaking my head back and forth.

"Calm down!" he urged, engulfing me in nothing but my sister's blood. It was only then that I knew it was Damien.

I couldn't breathe. I couldn't stop fighting. I was choking, drowning deeper in my despair. In the memories that would haunt me when I was awake and terrorize me when I tried to sleep.

"I hate you! I wish you were all dead!" I yelled hysterically. I was hyperventilating to the point where my vision was getting spotty. My vocal cords felt like they were on fire. "Don't touch me!" I screamed bloody murder, continuing my assault.

Hitting all over his face, his chest, anywhere I could with him still holding onto my flailing body. He didn't block me, he didn't stop me. He let me deliver every blow, exactly how he let Teresa. Knowing he deserved it and more.

"This is all your fault! You did this! Murderer!" I roared, pushing him and hitting him harder, faster, letting my adrenaline kick in at full force. My eyes seeing red, and my body sickened with rage and the desire to fall apart.

"You *puta*!" the man who I hit in between the legs sneered. Grabbing ahold of Yuly, trying to yank her out of my deathly grasp.

"NO! PLEASE NO!" I begged, gripping onto her as tight as I could. "She's all I have! PLEASE!"

Her dress tore and her arm snapped off, causing the men to laugh harder as I mourned another life that they were about to take away from me.

"PLEASE!" I bellowed out.

He was now holding onto Yuly as he looked me in the eyes, snapping her head from her body.

"NO!" I shouted loud enough to break glass, reaching for her before he threw her across the room.

As if she was nothing.

When she meant everything to me.

"I hate you! I hate you! I hate you, so much!" I sobbed, struggling against Damien's arms. Bringing my hands up to his neck, I scratched my nails down to his chest. Leaving a trail of blood in their wake. I needed to get to Yuly.

Damien forcefully threw me onto the floor like a rag doll, hitting my head with a thud. I shuddered from the impact of his strength.

"You fucking bitch!" Damien raged, looking down at me with hate in his eyes. His demeanor quickly changing. "Leave us, NOW! I'll take care of this little bitch!"

"I should fuck the disobedience right out of her," one of the men fumed, walking out the door with the other man. Leaving us alone.

"I said I got her! Now get the fuck out!"

Before I gave it another thought, Damien pulled his gun out from the back of his fatigues. It was then that another brutal reality came crashing down on me.

I. Was. Wrong.

So very wrong…

The monster hadn't left, he was standing right in front of me. Pulling the trigger.

Ending it all…

For me.

5
Damien

I didn't give it a second thought.

I grabbed a book of matches from the end table, striking the strip, watching the end spark. Taking a second to smell the sulfur before throwing the stick on the floor. Lighting the godforsaken house on fire. I was right, it only took seconds for the shitty, thin wood to catch fire. Orange and red flames crept over the massacre, igniting the blood, erasing the night like it never happened.

I took one last look at her small, lifeless body lying on the floor in front of me. Remembering the look in her eyes when my gun was aimed directly in her face, before she took her last breath. There was nothing I could do anymore.

What was done, was done.

This was my life…

Now, forever, and all the days in between.

I walked out of the house completely numb, as the flames erupted behind me. Engulfing the shack, burning the bodies of the loving family that once lived there.

Their blood eternally on my hands.

"What the fuck?" Salazar questioned, cocking his head to the side. He was leaning against his limo with my father and Pedro by his side. The other guards were already waiting inside the vehicle.

"Que?" I replied, *"What?"*

"La niña? ¿La mataste?" he asked, *"The girl? You killed her?"*

"You said she was my responsibility. What the fuck would I do with a little girl?"

"Damien, she was a child. You didn't need—" my father started.

"I didn't need to do what?" I interjected him, stepping up in his face for the second time that night. "I'm sorry, I don't know how any of this works. My father must have forgotten to mention he was a cold-blooded killer. Isn't this what you wanted? Training me all these years, preparing me to become a *soldier*? I did what I had to do. In my eyes, she was a fucking liability. You want her running her mouth to anyone who will listen? Because I sure as shit don't. I did her a favor, she's with her family now. It's where she belongs."

Salazar narrowed his eyes at me, grinning. "A saint one minute, a sinner the next. You see, Damien, you and I are not that different at all. You're such a loose fucking cannon—a wild card. I've always admired that about you. Never knowing what you're going to do. Keeps things interesting."

I eyed him up and down, repeating his words, "Fatherland or death, we shall win."

"You should have seen how he threw the little bitch down," Pedro chuckled. "We let you have your first kill to yourself, motherfucker, the way it should always be. But next time… we get to watch."

Emilio smiled, pushing off his limo. "It gets easier, just ask your father, but unlike him, you don't pick up strays," he chuckled, walking over to me, and I resisted the urge to ask him what he meant.

"I knew it wouldn't take long until you saw things my way. You're a true Cuban. A goddamn soldier, and I'm fucking proud to have you stand by me." Throwing his arm over my shoulder, he tugged me into his side. "This is only the beginning. Tonight was nothing compared to what I have in store for you. You will accomplish big things with my guidance. Before you know it, you'll be just like me. Everything you wanted, trained for, came true tonight, Damien," he affirmed, nodding to his men. "Now, let's get the fuck out of here and let these traitors rot in Hell, where they belong."

I stepped into the vehicle, taking a seat in the same spot I had when we arrived. Sinking into the black leather and leaning my head back against the headrest. I caught a glimpse of my face amongst the flames, reflecting off the tinted glass. No longer recognizing the man staring back at me, as I watched the house burn to the ground.

"How did it feel to have your first taste of pussy? Her virgin blood on your cock? She loved it. Don't let her fool you, I know you heard the *puta's* moans. A little advice for next time, it feels much better when you actually come," Salazar mocked, making everyone laugh right along with him. Except my father, he was lost in his thoughts. Staring out the tinted window.

I scoffed, "I guess unlike all the men in this limo, I can fuck for longer than five minutes."

They all laughed harder, throwing their heads back. Salazar handed me a bottle of bourbon and I greedily took it down, inhaling the burn of the fiery liquid with fucking pleasure. I wanted to forget. I wanted to pretend like tonight never happened.

Knowing it was far from fucking over.

I didn't know how much time went by before the limo came to a halt outside of my house. "Get some sleep. Got an early morning tomorrow. Be at my house by seven," Emilio instructed, breaking me from my trance-like state of emptiness.

I gave him a curt nod and stepped out, quickly realizing I was the only one to exit the vehicle as it drove away. I shook my head, unfazed. It wasn't unusual for my father to stay by Salazar's side, leaving me to fend for myself. Except this time, it had nothing to do with his duties and loyalty to our leader. He was purposely avoiding me.

Ashamed. Fully aware of the fucking monster in the making.

Me.

I shook off the thoughts, making my way inside. Setting what I had on the counter, I went straight into the shower, fatigues and all. Trying to rinse away the night's memories that would forever be a part of me. Letting the hot water burn into my skin, needing to feel something, anything, again. Watching all the blood from the lives I had taken swirl around the drain.

Out of sight, but it would never be out of mind.

After the water turned cold, I got out. Going about my business before jumping into my car and driving off into the night. It didn't take long until I reached my first destination, rushing up the front steps and knocking on the door. She answered immediately, looking confused.

"I need your help," I simply stated, handing over what I was carrying.

She didn't ask any questions, giving it back to me once she was done. I kissed her cheek and just as fast as I had arrived, I was gone.

The streets were dark and empty, and I welcomed the solitude. The storm in my mind had come and gone, but the wind remained as I drove down memory lane. I parked my car on the gravel path just after one in the morning. Turning off the engine, but leaving the headlights on to see through all the haze and dust falling from the night's sky.

I took a deep breath to steady my nerves before exiting my car. Making sure to grab what was sitting in my passenger seat, I tucked it in the back of my jeans, right beside my gun. The stench, lingering in the air immediately assaulted my senses, but I didn't pay it any mind. Too focused on the responsibility I still had. One foot in front of the other, I was pulled to my purpose. Hearing nothing but the charred debris beneath my boots and the wind whistling in the trees. Faint sounds of what was to come.

I never believed in having a bond with someone, never thought about fate or destiny or any of that bullshit. Never considered being tied to a soul through a connection that didn't make any sense. Though the second I stepped into that barn, I knew exactly where she'd be hiding.

As if her heart was now linked to mine.

I turned on the soft lighting, illuminating the open space of the decrepit structure. Stepping further into the barn to take a quick look around. It was fairly empty except for some old farming tools on the furthest wall and barrels of hay scattered throughout the area.

The ladder to the hay loft was lying partially broken on the ground. Like it had been kicked off the ledge it was once secured to, above my head. I couldn't help but chuckle as I set the intact part of the splintered wood against the nearest support beam, in the corner. Taking two steps at a time, I hoisted my six-foot-four frame up, clearing the missing space to climb up to the loft to get her.

An immediate sense of pride washed over me as I made my way up there. Another feeling that made no fucking sense to me. I had no idea who she was, but I already had an emotional attachment to her. Proud as fuck she was smart enough to try to derail anyone from coming to hurt her again. I moved a few barrels of hay out of the way, pushing them over the edge of the loft to clear the small space.

What I saw next hurt me in ways I didn't think were possible. Not after what I'd witnessed and participated in that night. She was sitting in the back corner with her knees pressed against her chest. Both arms tightly wrapped around her legs, caging in a few baby chicks on her lap. Holding a hammer in her grasp so fucking tight that her knuckles had turned white.

"Jesus Christ," I breathed out, taking in her father's dried-up blood all over her face and body. The way she wasn't moving, just sitting there like a scared little mouse. She hadn't peered at me once, staring blankly out in front of her.

Lost.

I opened my mouth to say something, anything, but I didn't know where to start. There was so much to fucking say, so many explanations and apologies to be made, but not nearly enough time for me to amend them. I was frozen in front of her, picturing the life she would never have. The years of memories that would forever haunt her. Any mistakes or regrets she may be feeling. It all came rushing over me, piling on top of my conscience. The weight suffocating me like I was being buried alive. The rage and adrenaline was still pumping through my veins, searing to the point of pain.

Hating myself even more for what I had done.

"Amira…" I coaxed, surrendering my hands out in front of me as I crouched down to her level. Needing her to understand I wasn't going to hurt her any more than I already had.

Nothing.

I could see the night flashing before her eyes with no end in sight. Every last second of it playing out in front of her with nowhere for her to hide this time.

"Amira, my name is Damien. Can you look at me please? I need you to look at me… Can you do that for me?"

She sucked in air, snapping out of her worst nightmare. Turning her attention to gaze at me, as if she just realized I was there with her. She immediately scooted back, further away from me and into the wall like she was trying to mold herself into the wood. Her lips wouldn't stop shaking, staring at me with wide, petrified eyes. She lifted her trembling hand in the air, showing me she had a weapon.

Her demeanor broke what was left of my fucking heart. Replicating with the image of her standing there traumatized in front of me, while her sister Teresa lay dead in my arms.

The life that was taken away from Amira so harshly, so violently, so fucking unfairly.

As if we both never left the scene of the crime.

"It's okay… remember? I told you to run into the barn and hide, and I'd come back for you."

She winced, shutting her eyes. Sinking deeper into the abyss where her mind had gone, fiercely shaking her head back and forth.

"Amira, tengo algo para ti, mira… Por favor, muñeca, ayúdame para que pueda ayudarte," I voiced, *"Amira, I have something for you, look... Please, doll, help me so I can help you."*

I didn't know what possessed me to call her that, but as soon as I said it, she slowly started opening her gaze like it brought back some sort of memory for her. Our eyes connected as I clutched onto her doll in the back of my jeans.

After she hauled ass from the house, out the back door where no one could see her run to hide, I grabbed the broken pieces of her doll and hid them under my fatigues. No one noticed, though why would they, I played the goddamn part perfectly.

Once I got home, I took a shower, mostly for her sake. The last thing I wanted was for her to see me in the same shape I was in before I left. Covered in her sister's blood. It didn't take me long to get to Rosarío's house so she could fix and clean up the doll. Making it look almost as good as new.

Amira cautiously watched as I pulled the doll from behind my back, slowly placing it in between us. This was my last bit of hope, silently praying she would know this was my way of extending some sort of olive branch to her.

Where she could meet me in the middle to try to mend the future of both our lives. I was going to be in her life, whether she wanted me to be or not.

It would just make things easier if she allowed it.

"Yuly?" she finally spoke. Her eyes welling up with fresh tears, not believing what she was seeing. The sight of the small doll restoring a little piece of what was left of her heart.

I nodded not knowing what else to say, or how to make any of this easier for her. The doll was the only thing I had from her previous life. It didn't make things right by any means, but I was hopeful it would provide her with a little comfort.

Something…

Anything…

For her to keep living.

Our eyes never strayed from one another as she hesitantly reached for the doll. Taking it out of my hands.

"Muñeca, I'm not going to hurt you," I sincerely stated in Spanish. "You're going to have to trust me."

She stared at me and then down at her doll with so much confusion in her stare. Unsure what to think or what to do. Searching Yuly for some answers. She had to realize that she had no choice. At the end of the day, I was her only hope. I'd drag her out of here kicking and screaming if I had to, and I think a part of her was already aware of that.

"We have to go."

I brought her attention back to me. "Where? Where do I go?" she whispered loud enough for me to hear.

"You let me worry about that." I stood, extending my hand for her to take.

Her glare shifted to my hand and then down to her lap where the baby chicks were still lying.

"They can come too," I answered her unspoken question. Ready to do whatever it took to get her the fuck out of there.

She peered back up at me, narrowing her eyes. Trying to figure me out. Put together the missing pieces of the puzzle that were spread right out in front of her. "You promise… you promise you're not going to hurt me? I'm safe with you? From the monsters…"

For the third time tonight, it felt like I took another bullet to my goddamn heart. So, I simply replied, "You're safe with me, Muñeca."

She nodded like she believed me, placing the chicks in the twine basket beside her. Not saying a word as she warily grabbed ahold of my hand to leave this place once and for all. I carried her on my back down the ladder, telling her to wait for me while I went back up to grab her basket of chicks.

She sat in the backseat holding her baby doll tight, shedding some more tears for the life she was leaving behind. Occasionally, our gazes would meet in the rearview mirror, and I'd offer her a slight smile for reassurance. She'd just wipe away some stray tears and go back to observing out the window. When we hit the main road out of fucking Hell, she finally let her exhaustion take her under.

I once again drove to the only home I'd ever truly known. Just after two in the morning, Rosarío opened the door startled, blinking away her sleepy haze. Being woken up by me for the second time that night. She took one look at me and then down to the little girl covered in dried-up blood, who was hiding behind my legs. Her face tucked into her doll and the baby chicks.

Rosarío didn't hesitate, instantly greeting, "Come in."

6

Amira

I followed Damien into the house he brought me to, trying to keep my tears at bay. Scared he was just going to leave me here with some strange woman and I'd never see him again. I didn't know why I felt such an emotional attachment to a man I'd only just met.

A complete stranger.

When he raised his gun up to my face for the second time tonight, for a split-second I thought he was really going to kill me. But he didn't. He moved his gun to the left and pulled the trigger, hitting the wall instead. Immediately rushing me out the backdoor to get away. Ordering me to run to the barn as fast as I could and stay there till he came back for me.

I didn't think twice about it. I ran through the open field that used to bring me so much happiness. Waiting for my papi to chase after me and tickle me to the ground. But those days were gone. The light burning inside me was snuffed out by evil. I didn't look back, I just ran until I was by myself in the barn. Watching the only home I'd ever known burn to a pile of ashes in front of my eyes.

I was scared.

I was alone.

I hated being alone.

I grabbed a hammer and the only flashlight we owned, not wanting to turn on the barn lights and attract unwanted attention. I gathered my favorite baby chicks in Mami's twine basket and used the ladder to go up and hide in the loft. Kicking it over before tucking myself behind a stack of hay, waiting. It was my second favorite hiding spot, often spending time up there when Papi was away. I waited for what felt like forever, trying to find comfort through my furry babies, but the images of the night wouldn't leave me alone.

A nightmare I couldn't wake up from.

Not now.

Not ever.

So, I just kept waiting, slipping into a dazed-like state, willing my eyes to stay open. The next thing I knew, a tall, shadowy figure was crouched down right in front of me. As if he appeared out of thin air. At first, I thought I was imagining him. It wasn't until I heard him call me *Muñeca* and say he had something for me, that I realized he was real. For some reason, the image of him at that very moment brought back the memory of when Papi said he had a gift for me.

There was kindness in his eyes again, his stare never wavering from mine as he slowly placed Yuly in between us. Showing me he'd fixed her, cleaned her up, making her look perfect again.

For me.

I believed him when he said I was safe in his care, which was why I didn't want him to go. I didn't want to be a scared little girl, taking on this new world alone.

In a way, he was all I had left.

I smelled the woman before I felt her crouch down in front of me on the couch, bringing me back to the present. She smelled like cookies and honey, reminding me of my mami.

"What's your name?" she asked softly.

"Amira," I whispered into my doll, unsure of my new surroundings.

"What do you have there, Amira? Can you show me?" she questioned in the softest voice, rubbing my back.

"Yuly."

"Oh, is that your doll's name? That's a beautiful name for such a beautiful doll. Are those your baby chicks too?"

I nodded.

"How old are you, Amira?"

"Nine."

"Wow, you're a big girl. Can you show me your face? Can I see your pretty eyes?"

I swallowed hard, shyly lifting my chin.

She slightly gasped. "I was right. You look like a princess. My name is Rosarío. Damien is my family, so do you know what that means?"

I shook my head.

"That means you're now my family too."

I glanced over at Damien where he was sitting on the opposite couch, draped over with his elbows resting on his knees. Watching us with an intense glare. His eyes shifted to Rosarío, nodding to me. Responding to my unspoken question in my mind.

I could trust her too.

"Amira, I just made some torticas de moron. Those are Damien's favorite. How about we get you washed up and in some nice, clean clothes. Then I'll warm up some food and pour a tall glass of milk for you. How does that sound?"

I extended my basket of baby chicks, silently asking her what to do with them.

She lovingly smiled, brushing a few strands of hair away from my face like Papi used to do. "Don't worry about your baby chicks, they will be right here when you get back. I promise."

My eyes locked with Damien's for a few seconds and he simply nodded, once again easing my worries.

He'd be here too.

She turned on the shower in the bathroom, helping me clean off all the blood from my hair and body. Making me feel comfortable and not so alone as she told me all about her life. Where she was born, how she knew Damien, her husband's name who had suddenly passed away. Telling me it didn't matter that he was gone because he would always live in her heart.

I liked her.

It was hard not to.

She left one of her nightgowns on the sink for me since I had no clothes, saying she was going to warm up my food so it would be ready when I finished up. I got dressed, staring into the floor-length mirror when I was done. The girl reflecting back at me looked different, older, less innocent and pure. I bowed my head, grabbing Yuly, and turned off the light before I stepped out in the hallway, not knowing where to go.

"Who is she, Damien?"

I followed Rosarío's voice down the hall, listening closely as I made each step.

"Don't ask questions you don't want the answers to, Rosarío."

"Then what? I didn't ask any questions when I helped you, fixing that doll and cleaning her up for you. Ignoring the fact that it was covered in blood. But now, you bring this little girl covered in blood to my home, in the middle of the night. What should I be asking?"

"I didn't know where else to take her. I'm at a loss here too."

"Who is she?"

I stopped behind the swinging doors to the kitchen, waiting to see where this conversation was going. I knew I wasn't supposed to eavesdrop, but I couldn't help myself. I had to know what was going to happen to me.

"She's my responsibility. She's mine," he declared, catching me off guard.

"In what sense?"

"She's not my daughter, Rosarío. You know me better than that. I don't fuck around with whores."

"Right now, I feel like I don't know you at all because all you're giving me is vague responses."

He sighed, taking a deep breath. "Did you know?"

"Did I know what?"

"Don't play fucking games with me!" Damien roared, slamming his hand down on what sounded like a table. Making me jump. "My father. Emilio Salazar... My goddamn future!"

"Shhh! You're going to frighten the girl. Keep your voice down and your temper in check. Something tells me she doesn't know about your short fuse and foul mouth yet."

He scoffed, "After what she's witnessed tonight, it's her memories that are going to frighten her. My temper and foul mouth are the least of her concerns. Now answer my question. Did. You. Know?"

She didn't say anything for what felt like a long time until she finally stammered, "Your father, he... he's... a good man, Damien..."

"In comparison to what? Eh?"

Silence.

He snidely chuckled. "Who doesn't know who now, Rosarío?"

"You knowing my past doesn't change that little girl's future. I would know, I've been in her shoes. You and your father are more alike than you—"

"Fuck him! To hell with him and his bullshit lies!"

"That's not fair."

"You want to know what's not fair? I'll tell you what's not fucking fair... what will happen to Amira if Salazar finds out I didn't really kill her? That's what's not fucking fair."

"What will happen to me?" I interrupted without thinking, stepping foot into the kitchen. Looking at Damien for answers like I'd been doing all night.

He didn't hesitate, responding, "The same fate that met your family tonight."

"But… he said… the monster… he said… he told you… that I was yours… you remember?" I stuttered, my voice trembling.

"No, Damien, that's where you're wrong," Rosarío countered, bringing our attention to her. "He'll use her as a pawn against you. Exactly how he did with your father."

"Is that what happened? He used you as a—"

"No. He didn't have to. He already had you," she interrupted Damien, pausing like she was thinking what to say next. "*Fatherland or death, we shall win, right?* You see, he doesn't just want your loyalty, he wants your soul. We're all prisoners here, it's why we live this communist life. He gets off on the power. The more you fight him, the harder he will come after you. I would know… it cost my husband his life."

"Rosarío—"

She stepped toward him, cutting him off again. Placing her hand on his cheek in a loving gesture. Adding, "But I wouldn't have had the pleasure to help raise you, if the circumstances were different."

The expression on Damien's face quickly changed. Suddenly understanding what she implied. Only confusing me even more.

She left him in a daze, walking over to where I stood, crouching down to my level. She smiled with tears in her eyes. "I'm so sorry, Mamita. I know what it's like to lose your world, when all your family wanted was to give you a better one. You're safe here from the monster, I promise."

I nodded, what other choice did I have.

I ate in silence at the kitchen table, overhearing them talk from the living room. Even though they were whispering, I could still hear Damien tell her that he would provide for me. Getting me all the things I needed from clothes, to food, to a tutor. She told him not to worry about any of that now, they would figure it all out in time together.

After devouring my plate of food, I set my dish in the sink, wanting to join them in the living room. When I walked in, my heart sank. Damien was nowhere to be found.

Rosarío was sitting, playing with my baby chicks. She wanted to give me a quick tour around her house, my new home as she called it. Trying to make me more comfortable and at ease with the new situation that was now my life. I barely paid her any attention.

He was gone.

He had left me.

He didn't even say goodbye.

She ended the tour by showing me where I could sleep, opening the door and turning on the light. It was much bigger than my room back home. A simple space with a twin bed, dresser, and some old paintings on the walls. A floral armchair sat in the far corner near the bed with a knitted throw blanket draped over the back and a little reading table beside it.

"I know it's not much right now, but you can make it your own. We can go out and get you some girly decorations, a comforter, and some toys to spruce up the space," she said.

I was at a loss for words, resisting the urge to cry again. I couldn't believe he'd left me. After all that, he abandoned me. My finger traced an old book with worn pages sitting on the little table.

"This was Damien's room when he'd stay with me."

I felt a sudden sense of comfort, learning that this was his room. Soothing the loneliness in my heart.

"I used to read that book to Damien every night at bedtime when he was a boy. Maybe I could read it to you sometime."

I just gazed at her, nodding. Unable to push through the sadness. She took one last look around before heading to the door. Reminding me that her room was just across the hall and I could come get her if I needed anything, no matter the time. I simply nodded again, exhausted and overwhelmed. Feeling like yet another person had already left my life.

She tightly hugged me, kissing the top of my head, and said goodnight. I took one last look around the room like she had and then went and used the bathroom down the hall, going about my business as if it was any other night. Brushing my teeth with the toothbrush Rosarío had left out for me and washing up. Avoiding the mirror at all costs.

I slightly opened the door to the bathroom when I was done. Peering out into the dark hallway, still unsure of my surroundings, before making my way back to my room. Clutching onto Yuly as hard as I could for comfort. As soon as I stepped inside, I stopped dead in my tracks when I saw him. Immediately wondering where he came from.

Damien.

He was standing in the middle of the room, holding the basket of chicks, waiting for me. I didn't know what came over me, but I breathed a visible sigh of relief and ran to him. Throwing my arms around his legs as tight as I could, not feeling so alone anymore. I couldn't hold back the tears any longer. Crying into his jeans, letting go of every last emotion I still had bottled up inside of me.

He was there.

He was really there with me.

I wasn't imagining it.

His arm wrapped around my shoulders, hugging me back. I squeezed him tighter. Sobbing harder.

"Shhh…Muñeca. I'm here. Shhh… It's okay, I'm here."

In that moment with him, something told me that for the first time in his life…

He didn’t feel so alone anymore either.

7
Damien

Four. Years.

Four fucking years since I faced the brutal reality of my fucked up life. The true meaning of what communism and our government stood for.

Corruption.

Salazar destroyed our nation and completely degenerated the Cuban people. He resented the upper crust who he believed sold their souls to *"Yankee capitalists."* Only serving the interests of the rich and oppressing the poor. He loathed everything the United States symbolized. Especially their capitalistic and imperialistic way of life.

Except, Emilio Salazar was an extremely intelligent and charismatic man. He targeted the poor and uneducated first, guaranteeing them free everything. *"I wanted what you had, but I didn't want to work for it,"* was his motto. Promising everyone equality was how he triumphed to begin with. Using the fact that the lower-class population was much larger than the middle and higher classes. Salazar knew they wouldn't know any better, so he took advantage. In their eyes, he was just the modern-day fucking Robin Hood, taking from the rich to give to the poor.

It was all a bunch of bullshit lies.

A fairytale you told a child at night.

The moment he stepped foot into office, all the wealthy, educated professionals fled Cuba. They found refuge in other countries, including the opposing side. The one country Emilio despised so damn much—the United States. Where they could still prosper and live their comfortable lifestyle they worked so hard for. Pretty much telling Salazar to go fuck himself. Fully aware that Cuba would turn to shit, with no social class regime.

Emilio Salazar's revolution was nothing but a revolution of envy.

His motive for everything stemmed from power. He thrived on control, using it over the less fortunate. In his eyes, everyone was beneath him. At his mercy. Sure, he wanted equality for all, but only if the *"all"* stayed where they belonged. On their goddamn knees, bowing to him. He was an egomaniac who hated his own people. There were no colors. There were no options. If you weren't his friend, you were his foe. If you weren't with him, you were against him.

Traitors, as he called them.

You had to become your own worst enemy in order to survive his hell.

Marching in line.

Following his orders.

Doing his fucking dirty work.

I was oblivious until I saw his true colors. By that time, it was too late to do anything. It was much easier to stand beside him than to betray him and pay with my life. I couldn't do that to Amira, she'd already lost too much. There was no way I'd let her lose me too.

So instead, I paid with my soul.

Condemned.

Monstrous.

At the end of the day, what other fucking choice did I have…

I was twenty-two-years-old with so much blood on my hands already. I was surprised I could still see my skin.

I killed.

I tortured.

I played fucking God while I was rotting in Hell.

Slaughtering men and women. Taking the lives of anyone Salazar said had to go. Yes, Emilio was my leader, but I wasn't up in the crevice of his asshole like everyone else was. Nor did I kiss it. He may have owned me in one way or another, but he didn't own my balls.

I still did what I had to.

Fulfilled duties on my own terms.

When I wanted, how I fucking wanted.

I drew the line at harming a child. I wouldn't so much as touch a hair on their heads. Not after Amira. Standing my ground, the first time I told him no, I thought he was going to put a bullet in my head, but instead I became his favorite. Probably reminding him we were one in the same. Everyone knew I was Salazar's main soldier and wasn't to be fucked with. Not many attempted to anyway. However, there was always that one motherfucker, here and there, who wanted to be top dog, and I had to set them straight.

I was alpha.

End. Of. Story.

I didn't take shit from anyone. Not even Emilio himself.

The offenses ranged from being as severe as someone plotting to take Salazar down, or as insignificant as a person telling me to go fuck myself. The punishment was always harsh though, no matter what the crime. It could range from death to torture, or plain imprisonment. No one disrespected me, I made sure of it. There were no imaginary lines. I'd crossed them all. No boundaries. No second chances. No redemption.

Not for me.

For them.

For anyone.

I planned and led ambushes against possible foreign attacks. Went on killing sprees. Raided homes, businesses, and even colleges, where he believed rebels were staked out. I orchestrated firing squads, ripping civilians from their beds in the middle of the night. Ordering them to face the wall so I could shoot them in their backs. Making it much easier to kill several traitors at once.

I witnessed and participated in it all.

Somewhere along the way in the last four years, I stopped allowing myself to feel, to think, to dream of another life. I became desensitized to it all. Now, I just did whatever I was ordered to do, without giving it a second thought.

Becoming as feared as Salazar himself.

The most fucked up part of it all was I took pleasure in it. The apple never falls far from the tree, and I was no fucking exception. You'd be surprised what the human psyche was capable of when it had no other choice. Only the strongest survived, and I would always make it out alive.

I didn't know darkness and evil lurked inside of me until I had to murder in order to thrive in this life. The control, the power, the sins of it all were just as addicting as they were afflicting. Consuming every last part of my being.

Becoming the fucking monster they trained me to be.

Inflicting mental torture on prisoners was a thing of the norm. A tactic I enjoyed participating in the most. For the last week, I'd spent my mornings with inmate, Vicente Reyes, prisoner 95708. He was sentenced to twenty years behind bars for killing a handful of Cuban soldiers. We needed the names of the men he orchestrated his terrorist attack with, and he had yet to provide us with even one.

I nodded to the prison guards as I made my way inside the interrogation room for the seventh straight day, dismissing them. Vicente was seated at the head of the long rectangular table, positioned in the middle of the room. Forgoing his usual seat on the side where he'd been sitting for our previous meetings. His glare immediately shifted from his shackled wrists to the box in my hands.

Waiting.

His curiosity becoming more evident with each passing minute. I knew what he was trying to do. Reading a suspect's body language was a talent I had perfected over the years. Nothing got pass me. The way his index finger on his right hand twitched slightly every few seconds. How his jaw was clenched as the muscles on his neck tensed. No matter how hard he tried to avoid it, I could see his pulse rapidly beating from the visible distance between us. Vicente wanted to come off all hard and unfazed, but I could smell his bullshit from a mile away. Although, I had to give credit where credit was due, the man had some brass fucking balls, sitting parallel to me.

He was trying to portray our interrogation as some sort of power struggle that day. I would be lying if I said I wasn't fucking amused by his disposition. The motherfucker hadn't been cooperating, not even with the electrocution or the depravation of food for weeks at a time. Making him starve until he was all skin and fucking bones. Fatigued as fuck from the daily beatings, the hard labor, and the solitary confinement.

None of it was working. So I decided to bring him a gift.

I grinned, placing my gun down on the table with the barrel pointing directly at him, setting the black box beside it. Nonchalantly unbuttoning my military jacket before taking a seat on the opposite side of him. I leaned back into my wooden chair, making myself comfortable. Noticing his eyes hadn't wavered from the package, not even for a second. I didn't pay him any mind, wanting the anticipation to build. Knock the motherfucker down a few notches before delivering my final blow.

"What did you think, Vicente? That you were going to be a brave soldier? Out to do away with the revolution? With Salazar? Attempting to go against your government, against your country. Against your own people… Killing true soldiers who *were* fighting for their revolution."

He didn't hesitate, confessing, "Absolutely. I'd do it again, if I had another chance," he spat with a sadistic grin spread across his face.

I leaned into the table, arching my eyebrow with my hands clasped together out in front of me. "A real man would've gotten the job done the first time. He wouldn't need another chance."

He shrugged, biting his lower lip.

"Your anti-communistic way of life didn't do shit for you, except land your ass in prison. You're a poor excuse of a man. You failed everyone, Vicente. The conspirators you organized this attack with, your régime." I paused, allowing my words to sink in. "Not to mention your family."

"My fami—"

"You're nothing but a disgrace to our country. To your children's children. I highly doubt your kids could even look upon their old man with pride in their eyes, knowing he's a fucking failure. Rotting behind bars. Your parents are probably rolling over in their graves in shame."

His fists clenched, his nostrils flared, and his face paled. My words clearly affecting him, far worse than any physical torture I could ever inflict. My job was to demoralize Vicente, a task I executed with joy. Breaking a man lifted me in ways I never thought possible. It empowered my rage, making me feel like fucking God. Superior to him and all the others who attempted attacks against our country.

"I did… I'm… that's not…" he stammered, unable to form a coherent sentence. His ego eating him alive.

"You've done your country wrong, Vicente. It's a good thing there's no mirrors in this hell hole. I'd hate to be you and have to look at myself every fucking day, knowing I'm nothing but a piece of shit. The bottom of the barrel. Fuck, it all makes sense now, no wonder why your wife didn't put up too much of a fight. She'd been waiting for a real man to come along all her life."

He jerked back, breathing out, "My wife?" His manic thoughts taking over.

I slid the box across the table, hitting his arm that was resting on the surface; it stopped a few inches away from his face. His head flew back startled, locking eyes with me. I could see his anxiety radiating off him, fueling the fiend inside of me.

He swallowed hard, holding his chin up higher. Acting unfazed.

Provoking me.

"I bring you a gift, and I have yet to hear you thank me," I mocked in a condescending tone, breaking the sudden silence.

"A gift?" he asked, narrowing his eyes. Confused and overwhelmed all at once.

"Did I stutter? Go ahead, open it."

He hesitated for a moment before reaching out his trembling hands to grab the box. The panic dwelling inside of him with each passing second. No longer the tough son-of-a-bitch he once portrayed.

As he started to lift the lid, I added, "Someone once told me the only way to make a man pay for his sins was through the ones he loved the most."

"What the fuck?" he murmured in shock, grabbing the severed female finger from the box. Immediately recognizing the wedding band prominently on display.

His mouth quivered, and his body shook. I saw him swallowing down the bile rising in his throat. I imagined the memories of his wedding day were too much for him to bear. The emotions from seeing his beautiful bride walking down the aisle were flooding back. I could see it in his eyes, it was one memory right after the other. It was crazy how much significance one small finger could have. He was visibly shutting down.

It was time to break him entirely.

"I know how much you miss her. Aren't you going to thank me now?"

His chest heaved with anger as he threw the finger back into the box and shoved it away. Quickly making the sign of the cross with his shackled wrists.

I stood, placing my hands in my pockets. Casually making my way over to him. “The only god in this room, is me. Now confess the names I want, or I’ll be paying your wife another visit. Only next time, it will be her fucking head in that box.”

“Maria… no… please, God, no…” He bowed his head with the shame and regret I wanted him to feel.

“Don't worry, she didn't scream too much,” I sympathized, leaning forward close to his ear. “Not with my cock in her mouth.”

“You motherfuc—”

I crudely gripped onto his throat, jerking him backward in his chair. Slamming his body onto the ground near my boots. I held him down. “That’s the thanks I get for bringing you a piece of your wife?”

He instantly grasped onto my hand, kicking his legs out from under him. I choked him harder, placing my knee on his sternum, squeezing the air right out of him. His face turned red and his eyes began to water as his life was being drained out of him.

By me.

“Someone needs to learn some goddamn manners, and lucky for you…” I hovered close to his face. “I’m just the man to teach you.” And with that I cold-cocked him, knocking him the fuck out.

He came to when I was dragging his soaking wet body, by his collar, out of the lake behind the prison. Convulsing, sucking in the air I was ruthlessly denying him. Choking on the water that took up occupancy in his throat and lungs. Spitting up god knows what. He staggered to find his balance, falling to his knees on the murky shore. His hands being cuffed behind his back, along with his ankles, didn’t help his current predicament.

I ignored him as he visibly struggled, trying to get loose. Confused by the turn in events. Still not realizing he wasn’t going anywhere unless I wanted him to. There was nowhere else I’d rather have him than at my mercy. I waited until he tired himself out. Until there was no fight left in him, and all he could do was roll over and play fucking dead. I was used to the hysteria that came along with my violent acts. It was all part of the job.

I leaned forward, close to his ear again. Cocking my head to the side, I rasped, "Give me the names."

He heaved, his chest rising and falling with each second that passed. Desperately trying to regain his breathing and stay conscious.

"I didn't hear you," I taunted. This time grabbing ahold of his neck, shoving just his face back into the water. Holding him under as his body fought to get free.

As I hauled him back up, he choked out, "My Lord and Savior!"

I viciously smiled, bringing his face right in front of mine to glare into his eyes. "How's that working out for you? Where the fuck is he now?"

His dark pools met mine, spewing, "You're going to rot in Hell for this."

"I'm already there, motherfucker."

"I did what I had to do! I killed those soldiers for the good of our people! Anyone who stands by Emilio Salazar deserves to die!"

"Is that right?" I chuckled, dragging him back under the water. Holding him down longer that time. Watching his air bubbles come few and far between. I waited, not allowing the traitor to die. Drowning him over and over again to the brink of death, till his body pleaded with me to end it all.

"Please…" he whispered, trying to catch his breath.

"Please, what?"

"Please… have compassion…"

"Compassion for a man who murdered five of my men? Eye for an eye, motherfucker. You reap what you sow. You have one last chance to confess names, or my next stop will be your house. I'll just wait till your daughters are home this time. I always wanted to fuck sisters," I deviously chuckled, feeling his heart pounding against my grip on his neck. His nostrils flared while his mind reeled with uncertainty. "Count with me, one… two… times up!"

"Maur… his name is… Maur… Mauricio! His name is Mauricio Gonzalez!" he screamed out then spit in my face.

I abruptly let him go, causing him to sink further into the water. He froze, waiting for my next move. I looked him in the eyes and nodded toward the guard, silently ordering him to get out of my face.

"Are you—"

"If I wanted to have a conversation, I would've asked you a question. Go!"

He breathed a sigh of relief, cautiously backing away from me, getting out of the water. Turning around once he was on the shore and walking toward Federico, the guard.

At the last second, I called out, "Vicente!" He spun back around as I slowly wiped his spit off my cheek with the back of my hand. His eyes instantly widened, realizing what I was now holding.

Tilting my head to the side with dark and dilated eyes, I reminded him, "You never fucking thanked me." Pulling the trigger, I blew his head off.

Splattering his blood and brains behind him in the sand. Immediately taking him to join all the other souls I collected in this very place.

"Another one? Jesus, man. Can't we keep any of them alive?" Federico nonchalantly laughed.

"Someone had to teach him some manners," I stated as I made my way out of there. It was close to dinnertime, and I needed to get to Amira before six; that was our daily routine more often than not.

This motherfucker made me lose track of time, and I hated to keep her waiting. Worrying something bad may have happened to me. She was the only light in my life, but she wasn't a little girl anymore. No longer a child I could lie to. She was thirteen, and the older she got, the easier it was for her to read through my bullshit excuses. I started to make it a point that the only time she saw me was when I knew my demons were at bay.

When I could be the person she needed. The one who saved her, took care of her, and protected her. Yet to acknowledge that I was one of the men who tore her world apart. She was expecting me, but I was taking a gamble on who would show up for her. I contemplated that before I even got into my car.

Amira was the only penance I had.

Eternally battling the hell I was already burning in.

8

Amira

I sat on the ledge of my reading nook in the living room, with my back against the comfy pillows and Yuly at my side. Failing miserably to stay focused on the task at hand. Homework. My mind dancing from one random thought to another.

"Amira, Mamita, you've sat by that window every evening at five o'clock for the past four years. Do you really think I believe you're studying?" Rosarío asked with humor in her tone.

I smiled sweetly, peering up at her. "I am studying, Mama Rosa. I just happen to like sitting in the sun while I do so."

She nonchalantly nodded to the window beside me, stating the obvious, "It's raining and gloomy out today."

"Oh, yeah... I knew that. This is just my routine. You know how I am, a creature of habit. I like things to stay consistent and stuff. That's all."

She arched an eyebrow, cocking her head to the side. "I may be old, but I'm not stupid, Amira. I know you're waiting for Damien. You claimed that as your spot since the first day Damien brought you home. Why do you think he built this nook for you? He knows you will always be waiting for him. It brings him comfort."

I smiled wider. It brought me comfort waiting for him too. Damien built the space for me three years ago for my tenth birthday, after he caught me waiting for him by the window one evening. It was a cozy little niche with a cushioned bench that overlooked the front yard. It quickly became my favorite place to curl up with a blanket and pretend to study. This time, I had my English dictionary open in my lap, pretending to practice the words my tutor, Charo, assigned me to work on over the weekend. Absentmindedly trying to remember the last word I read for the tenth time, but I couldn't.

My mind was somewhere else entirely.

"You're not old. You're only forty-two. And you're beautiful, Mama Rosa. You don't look a day over thirty."

"Oh, bless your heart, sweet child. Wise beyond your years, I tell you. Though I hate to be the bearer of bad news, Mamita, but Damien may not come today."

"He'll be here. He comes most days, and besides, he always tells me when he can't because of work," I said, cringing at the fact that Damien still had to work for the monster.

She smirked, shaking her head. "Whatever you say. Finish up your day-dreaming about Damien, and go get washed up for dinner. I made your favorite." Rosarío kissed my forehead and walked out of the living room, whispering something under her breath I couldn't make out.

To be fair it wasn't only Damien preoccupying my thoughts. All of a sudden, I was feeling nostalgic. For some reason that day, I couldn't help but remember how the first year had been the hardest for me here. How adjusting to my new life without my family was an experience I never imagined I would have to go through. Damien spent every second he could, keeping me company. He stayed with me as much as possible, making sure I was well cared for mentally, physically, and emotionally. Doing his best to tend to my needs, wanting to make the transition easier on me. He was the best listener too. I couldn't count how many nights he spent with me on the porch swing out back, letting me tell him about my happy memories, or vent when I needed to. Though every time I talked about my family, I could see the pain in his kind eyes, and just as quickly as it appeared, he would blink and it would be gone.

As much as I opened up to him about my family, he never let me in on his feelings. He had the perfect façade in place for four years now. It was like he had built a wall around his emotions concerning that night. There were no cracks, no slips. Nothing could bring it down, not even me. I knew deep in my heart he felt responsible for my family's death. He carried this guilt around with him that weighed heavy like a wooden cross on his back. No matter how I saw it, the reality of the situation was, in his mind…

Their three lives.

Their three souls.

Were a burden he would forever carry on his own.

The night Damien entered my life was the best and worst day of my existence. I owed a lot to him for saving me. I knew he didn't believe it or even understand it, but I never blamed him for my family's deaths.

Not once.

It wasn't his doing, he didn't orchestrate it. Emilio did. Damien played a part, but the alternative would've led to his death, and if he had died, I would have died too.

So, he played the monster's game, and we both made it out alive.

Since then, Damien was a pillar in my life. He provided me with a safe and affectionate home, with a loving woman who was now like a mother to me. Rosarío always made me feel wanted and cared for as if I was her real daughter. From the moment I stepped foot into her house, she loved me. Always being there to comfort me when I needed to talk about my feelings or just cry. Which was typically over a big bowl of ice cream to drown my sorrows. She was adamant that food made everything better.

Both of them would make me laugh and smile on a daily basis. Giving me hope when all I had was despair. They were the only two people I had left in this world. They meant everything to me. As the days turned into weeks, and the weeks turned into months, and the months turned into years, I realized what Rosarío had told me the night we first spoke, couldn't have been more accurate. They were my family now. They truly were the best thing that could have happened to me, after losing my own.

Damien would spend the night at Rosarío's often, instead of going back to his apartment. Somehow knowing I'd need to see a familiar face in the middle of the night, when my dreams turned into nightmares. He'd lay with me, playing with my hair or rubbing my back until I fell asleep again. Sometimes he couldn't be here though, off fulfilling his obligations to the monster. On those nights, Rosarío would take his place, warming me up a glass of milk as I tried to shake off the emotions that my bad dreams usually evoked. Neither of them ever made me feel bad about disturbing their sleep, though.

I hadn't seen or heard from Emilio Salazar or any of his men since the night he murdered my entire family. Damien made sure to cover all the tracks, going as far as telling Rosarío's neighbors and friends that I was her niece. Later in private, letting them know that my parents had unexpectedly died in a fire and she was now my guardian. Wanting to prevent any emotions the truth may invoke in me. I don't know how Damien did it, but within the first few weeks he was able to provide me with a whole new identity. The only part of my past that remained the same was my name.

Amira.

He said it was the one thing he couldn't take away from me. As far as Emilio and his men knew, I burned in the fire right alongside my family that night, and I guess in a way, I had. Damien didn't just save me, he gave me a whole new life. One I would've never had the chance to live before. I had the best tutors and an education most people dreamed of, learning subjects I didn't even know existed. I also had the nicest clothes, from dresses, to pants, to blouses and t-shirts. It was endless. Damien never allowed me to want for anything. Neither did Rosarío.

"Amira, I'm going to walk over to Carmen's for a bit. She needs help with her torticas de moron," Rosarío shouted from the kitchen. "Please go get cleaned up! Oh, and check on dinner while I'm gone!"

"I will, Mama Rosa! I promise!" I yelled back as the side door shut behind her.

It didn't take long after she left for Damien to pull into the driveway. I smiled, big and wide as he parked his car next to Rosarío's, turned off the engine, and grabbed something from his passenger seat. Instinctively knowing it was probably something for me. I watched as he stepped out onto the pavement with a new doll firmly in his grasp, silently giggling to myself, I was right. He started bringing me gifts the day after I innocently shared that my papi use to do the same when he was away for work. Damien hadn't realized I was thirteen and getting a little too old for dolls. But I would never tell him that.

The sentiment behind his reasoning being too important to him.

He leaned against the hood of his car, looking down at the ground, as if he needed a minute to gather himself before coming into the house. His long, curly hair hid his deep-set hazel eyes that always held so much emotion behind them. Over the years I'd grown to read what he was thinking, feeling, expressing all at first glance. He closed his eyes, shaking his head, and pushed off the car to walk toward the front door.

I would be lying if I said it didn't seem like there were two sides to Damien. The man he was with *us*, and someone else entirely when he wasn't. His personality was extremely somber and serious most of the time. Probably stemming from being a soldier and being raised by one too. His whole demeanor screamed military man, even the way he walked was stocky and abrasive.

Damien didn't like to be teased, as harmless as it may be. He could do the teasing, but the second you turned it around on him, it was a different story. He'd get all butt-hurt about it, which only provoked me to do it more. I would mimic his stride when I knew he was watching me, just to make him laugh. I'd stand tall with my arms straight at my sides and a stern look on my face.

He'd try not to laugh until I would imitate his deep voice, saying random things like, "*Hi, my name is Damien and I walk around like there's a stick up my butt. I have no sense of humor. And all I want is for Amira to study, so she has the best education and grows up to be the smartest woman in the world. But she's already smarter than I am, I just haven't admitted it out loud yet.*"

My teasing usually ended with him tickling me to the floor. Always using the fact that he was much bigger than me to his advantage. I'd call him a bully, and he'd call me a brat.

Rosarío would always reprimand me for acting silly and making fun of Damien, but I could see it in her eyes; she actually enjoyed seeing him laugh or smile because of my antics. Only confirming what I knew all along without me ever having to ask her. She'd been waiting all his life for someone besides her to care about him enough, to know there was more to him hidden beneath the fatigues, or what he thought he needed to be.

Whatever that was.

I jolted when I heard the front door slam a little harder than usual. Immediately looking down at the dictionary in my lap. Damien wanted me to be multi-lingual just like him. I was learning English, French, Portuguese, Italian, and Spanish. I thought I spoke Spanish correctly, so when Damien politely said it wasn't the proper or educated way of speaking, I was a little embarrassed. I knew he wasn't trying to hurt my feelings, he was aware the school I attended in El Campo wasn't anywhere near as skilled as the tutor he hired for me. Charo was one of the most elite in Santiago—a sweet, older woman who reminded me a lot of Rosarío. Her hair was always pulled back in a bun, smelling like fresh baked goods. She studied in a European boarding school. A place where nuns lived, a monastery is what she called it.

Damien was very intense about my schooling, always expressing how important it was for me to have the finest education. Constantly encouraging me to reach above and beyond what was standard in knowledge, aptitude, and life in general. Saying it would make me a well-rounded young lady, which he felt Cuba needed more of.

Damien's boots pounded against the floorboards with each step he took through the house. I sat up tall, smiling, eagerly waiting for him to enter the living room and greet me in whatever language he wanted to practice that day, like he always did. But instead, he walked in and tossed the doll on the couch near me, not saying a word. My smile quickly faded as soon as I looked up from my studies to meet his gaze, and he suddenly turned his back to me.

Leaving the room without so much as acknowledging me for the first time ever and made his way toward the kitchen.

I jerked back, confused.

Did I do something wrong? Was he mad that I wasn't really studying?

I waited for a few seconds before I stood and grabbed my new doll, following after him. Anxiously needing to know what was going on, thinking maybe I misinterpreted things. Nothing about the way he was acting was normal. I slowed my pace the closer I got to the kitchen, each step calculated and precise. My heart was racing a mile a minute, the closer I got to crossing the threshold into the unknown. Never in a million years did I ever expect to encounter…

The other side of Damien Montero.

9
Amira

When I walked through the swinging doors, he was standing in front of the stove with his back to me.

I didn't waver. "Hey, tout va bien?" I asked in French, *"Hey, is everything alright?"* Trying to maintain our normal, calm routine. Silently hoping it would make him smile, knowing he loved it when I showed him how much I was perfecting another language.

"Amira, how many times do I have to tell you not to leave the fucking stove on?" he snapped in a tone he had never used with me before.

I winced, completely caught off guard by his demeanor. "I didn't… Mama Rosa did. She went—"

"I don't give a fuck where she went!" He slammed the wooden spoon on the counter, causing his back to tense and his muscles to constrict.

My eyes widened, and my body jolted again. Stunned by the drastic turn of events with his dominant, demanding, controlling presence looming over the stove.

"When I tell you to do something, I expect you to fucking listen to me," he ordered in an eerie tone, making my lip quiver and my body tense.

I shook my head back and forth. "I… I … I do. I al—"

He abruptly turned around, rendering me speechless and was over to me in three strides, ripping the doll out of my hand. Still not fully looking at me, he spewed, “I don’t want to hear your bullshit excuses. You can’t do anything right, can you? Your pronunciation is horrible, have you even been studying? I’m not paying to have the most prestigious tutor in Cuba, if you’re going to fuck off!”

“Damien…” I gasped, taken back.

Where was the person I would catch up on every last detail of my day with? The man who seemed to look forward to our conversations as much as I did, like they were the best part of his day too. Where he’d nod his head or grin when I’d say something amusing, which was often. All while he listened intently to everything I had to share. It didn’t matter how trivial or unimportant it was. It meant something to him, because it meant something to me.

And to a thirteen-year-old girl, *that* meant everything.

I wanted him to fully face me. Look into his eyes like I had done so many times before, knowing they would show me everything I needed to see. But I was terrified of the man who’d be staring back at me. Adrenaline and fear surged through my veins. The thought alone caused shivers to course down my spine. I shuddered at the mere thought of making that connection.

“What?!” he roared, flexing his hands into fists at his side. His knuckles turning white from the pressure of his grip.

I should’ve run out of the room, but the expression on his face held me captive to the ground beneath me.

“Jesus Christ, Amira. Were you this needy with your papi? Always up his ass, begging for more fucking attention? Don’t I give you enough of that already? All I do is provide for you! Bring you gifts, help you study, put food on the table, and a roof over your head. I’m exhausted tending to all your needs! It’s like I’m raising a child, and I didn’t even fucking get laid! I didn’t ask for this life!” he viciously spat, stepping toward me. I instinctively stepped back in fear, only fueling his fury. “And you still haven’t fucking thanked me for your gift! Why don't you just go run along and play with all your precious goddamn dolls that I've paid for."

He threw my new doll at my feet, and I couldn't hold back any longer. "Oh my God! Who are you?" I blurted, already knowing the answer.

His gaze finally met mine, except it wasn't his kind eyes staring back at me.

They weren't familiar.

They weren't comforting.

They. Weren't. Damien's.

I wasn't just imagining it. It wasn't a figment of my mind. I'd never seen this stare before, at least not on him. They were dark and daunting, empty and evil. Only reminding me of the man who took my life away.

The monster…

"Better yet," he added, cocking his head to the side. Narrowing his deviant gaze at me. "Why don't you go run and hide. That seems to be the only thing you're fucking good at."

The forceful blow from his words almost knocked me on the floor, I felt like I couldn't breathe.

Winded from his actions.

Choking from his words.

All the air from my lungs ceased to exist, evaporating from the pain.

"I'm sor—"

"Now!"

I did.

I ran on pure emotion and terror, unable to get away from him fast enough. Trying to seek shelter anywhere I could. I didn't even realize where I was running to until I tried to open the front door. Only to have it unexpectedly slammed shut from behind me.

"Amira—"

I didn't have to wonder who it was. Not allowing him to get another malicious word out, I took off again. Running toward my bedroom this time. I barely made it five strides down the hallway before he grabbed ahold of my arm, hauling me backward to face him.

Instinctively, I fought to get free. "Let go!" I shouted, struggling to get away from him, but he wasn't having it. He grabbed my other wrist, tugging me forward, making me lose my footing. Slamming me into his hard chest. "Stop it! You're scaring me! Please, just stop it!" I pleaded, my trembling voice breaking with each word that left my mouth.

"Fuck," he breathed out, instantly letting me go.

I stumbled, tripping over my feet, trying to regain my balance, when a strong arm wrapped around my waist. Catching me before I face-planted into the wall. Damien held me steady.

"Muñeca," he immediately coaxed in a familiar voice, like he knew I desperately needed to hear it. Causing me to intuitively peer up at him through my lashes.

We locked eyes.

Neither one of us said a word, we didn't have to. The intensity surging through our connection in that moment was as captivating to him as it was to me. We were both standing there, breathing profusely. My heart pounding so hard in my chest that I swear he could hear it. Both of us lost in our own thoughts.

He knew what I was doing.

What I was looking for.

What I needed to see.

Only adding to the plaguing emotions that were placed in between us. A hint of darkness still remained in his honey-colored stare as if he was trying to break through the demons haunting him.

Battle his way back to me.

It seemed like seconds, minutes, hours went by where our silence spoke volumes even though nothing escaped, our lips. I could physically feel his thoughts raging war in his mind with no end in sight.

When he opened his mouth to say something, the front door opened, cutting him off, and Rosarío walked in. "I'm sorry I took so long. You know Carmen, once she starts talki—" She stopped dead in her tracks, taking in the scene in front of her. "What's going on?" she questioned, glancing from him to me, down to his hands that were still holding onto me.

I didn't hesitate, shoving off his chest, breaking his grasp on my hips, and stepping back and away from him, blurting, "Ask this imposter, maybe he won't treat you like you're nothing but a burden."

He grimaced. It was quick, but I saw it. With that, I spun around and left, walking back to my room.

"Amira, what—"

"Let her go, Rosarío. Just let her be," I overheard Damien interrupt her, as I slammed my door shut behind me.

Once it was closed, I leaned against the cool wood, taking a solid, deep breath. Refusing to cry, even though I was beyond hurt and confused. The fear I felt subsided, replaced with something I never felt before. I don't know how long I sat there, dazed and confused by his behavior.

Did he really mean those things? Was I too needy? Did I not do anything right?

I crept up off the floor with my heart aching and my mind burning. My reflection in my vanity mirror only made me sadder. I peered around the room at all the dolls on the shelves that he had gifted me over the years. Along with the shelves lined with nothing but books of stories that use to bring me so much happiness. There wasn't one thing in this room that Damien hadn't given me.

"All I do is provide for you! I'm exhausted tending

to all your needs! I didn't ask for this life!"

His cruel, but true, words echoed in my mind. *He didn't ask for this life...*

He didn't ask for *me*.

I was his obligation, and that was the harshest reality of all. I took one last look around the room before I grabbed a bag from under my bed and threw it on the comforter. Opening my drawers and closet, only grabbing a few necessities I would need. My eyes blurred with tears every time I shoved another piece of me into the suitcase. Thinking how I would never see him or Rosarío again.

"All I do is provide for you! I'm exhausted tending to all your needs! I didn't ask for this life!"

I repeated it over and over again in my mind, letting it sink into my soul. Fueling my determination to leave them both behind. I didn't know where I would go, but I wouldn't stay somewhere I wasn't wanted.

It wasn't fair to him.

To either of them.

I zipped my bag and pulled it off the bed, quietly opening my bedroom door to get to the bathroom, and grab a few last things.

"Damien, you have to stop blaming yourself for what happened. Amira knows it wasn't your fault," Rosarío declared, stopping me mid-stride as I was about to walk into the bathroom.

I tip-toed down the hallway, hiding behind the wall. Peering through the crack of the kitchen's swinging doors so they wouldn't know I was eavesdropping. I still hadn't learned I wasn't supposed to do that.

He scoffed, shaking his head while he stood in front of her. Rosarío was sitting in one of the island chairs.

"Only because she doesn't know any better. I fucking lost my shit on her today, Rosarío. I screamed at her. I scared her. I was maliciously cruel for no fucking reason, other than the fact that I couldn't shut it off. The *man* I am, the *same* man I vowed to never let her see," he countered, disgusted with himself. He started to pace the kitchen floor, tugging his hair back away from his face in a frustrated gesture like he wanted to rip it out. "I fucked up. I should've never come over tonight. I fucking knew it, but I was selfish. I wanted to see her. I needed to see her."

"Damien, that's not you. She knows that's not—"

"That. Is. Me," he argued, halting in place and sternly looked over at her. "What do you think I do every day, eh? You know whom I serve. You know what I am. Don't play dumb, Rosarío, you're no fucking good at it."

"Did you ever stop and think that you aren't like them? That you—"

"You mean before or after I took part in murdering her family?" he callously relayed, leaning against the counter with his arms folded across his chest. The impact of his words caused me to wince back in pain. His revelation and guilt weren't a surprise to me, but it still hurt to hear him admit it out loud.

"You know it as much as I do… She's not a little girl anymore. The older she gets, the more she's going to learn the truth. One day soon, I won't be the man who saved her. I'll just be another fucking monster that haunts her dreams."

I grimaced, not expecting him to say that. His response made my heart hurt for him. Probably in the same way his heart always hurt for mine.

Rosarío sighed, taking a deep breath. "She was never a little girl, Damien. She's already seen and gone through too much for her age. It's made her grow up faster. But you want to know what I see? I see her laugh and smile with you, more than I ever do with anyone else. Including *me*. She plays, she runs, she acts like the carefree young girl she's supposed to be. When she's with you… she feels safe. That girl doesn't hate you for anything, it's the exact opposite. She loves you, and you love her too. You love her so much that it terrifies you that one day, she may not look at you the same way. Not because you're a monster, but because you made her think you're one by pushing her away."

He didn't hesitate, his kind eyes shifted toward the door I was hiding behind. Like he could sense I was standing there the whole time. "Muñeca, if you're going to eavesdrop, you should make sure your shadow can't be seen under the doors."

I groaned, feeling apprehensive that I got caught, but I quickly shook it off. Confidently walking into the kitchen to face them. Both their eyes simultaneously went to the bag I was holding in my hands. The realization of what I was going to do swiftly replaced the concerned expressions on their faces.

Damien didn't falter, not that I expected him to. "How far do you think you would've made it, Muñeca, before I found you? You think I would ever let you walk out that door? Let you leave so that something bad happens to you? I couldn't live with myself, knowing I was the cause. For four years, I've made it a point to never let anything harm you. You're mine, Amira. My responsibility. I can't imagine you'd think I would ever allow you to run away. You have to know that. Tell me you know that."

I nodded, overwhelmed with emotion from how much he was sharing with me for the first time.

"I need to hear you say the words, Amira. Tell me you know that?" he demanded in a soft tone.

"I do. I know that." And I did… I always had.

He took a deep breath, the worried expression on his face slowly fading away.

"What happened to you tonight? Why did you say those things to me? Do you mean them?" I asked before I lost the courage, not knowing what I wanted him to answer the most.

I saw it in his stare that he wanted to lie to me. "I had a shitty day, before running into Emilio on my way here. He started to ask questions about Rosarío," he openly confided.

Suddenly shaking, I asked, "Do you think he knows that I'm—"

"No."

"But if he's—"

"Amira, do you trust me?"

"Of course," I firmly replied.

"Then trust me when I say today had nothing to do with you," he sincerely voiced, replying to my other question in his own subtle way.

"Damien nor I would ever let anything happen to you. Emilio is just being a nosy bastard. That's all. Nothing more, nothing less. Mamita, this is your home. We are your family," Rosarío stated, her eyes welling up with fresh tears, just thinking about what I was going to do. Making me feel worse. "Sometimes people say things they don't really mean. Families fight. And that's what we are, Amira. We're a family. We don't turn our back on one another. No matter what."

She was right.

The good.

The bad.

The love…

They were all part of being a family.

Damien's eyes promptly connected with mine.

And there he was…

My Damien.

"You scared me," I murmured loud enough for him to hear. "I thought… I thought I'd lost you too. To *him.*"

He grabbed the doll he brought home for me off the counter. Extending her out for me to take. Immediately reminding me of the night he saved me and every night since.

"Muñeca, I'm so sorr—"

Before he could finish his apology, I ran to him. Throwing my arms around his waist, hugging him as tight as I could. There were just some things that were better left unsaid, and this was definitely one of them. Right then and there, I promised myself that I would never let him scare me like that again. No matter how many times he tried. Now knowing, deep in my heart, that Damien needed me just as much I needed him.

Mi familia.

When he wrapped his protective arms around me and placed a kiss on the top of my head, I expressed, "I love you," for the first time into the side of his chest. Feeling as though he needed to hear me say it, more now than ever before.

It was only then I truly understood why Damien never asked me about my nightmares…

He didn't have to.

He lived them too.

10

Damien

"Ricardo and his men should be here soon. You ready?" Emilio questioned, as I took my seat beside him at the conference table.

We were about to have an important meeting in one of the nicer warehouses Salazar owned in downtown Santiago. Emilio had his dirty fucking hands in everything from guns, to drugs, to prostitution. When it came to Emilio Salazar, there wasn't anything he didn't own or operate. He knew it all but stayed hidden behind the scenes, orchestrating illegal shit like the puppet master he was. Transporting drugs from country to country with some of most wanted criminals around the world. The possible language barriers never mattered. As soon as Emilio chucked a stack of bills onto the table, suddenly everyone fucking understood each other.

Police, lawyers, the law in general, were all a joke. Pieces of paper he could wipe his ass with. They were all shady as fuck, tucked in his back pocket exactly where he wanted them. It was the small-time shit he involved himself in just for shits and giggles. Another thing to pass his time.

I simply nodded.

"He's an old colleague of mine, you know. This is the first time we'll be doing business in forty plus years. He lives in Colombia now, and has ties to all the important people over there. This is huge for us. Do you understand me?"

I nodded again. Mostly because I understood more than he knew.

What really got Salazar's cock hard was politics. Which was precisely where the biggest corruption existed to begin with. Ricardo was no exception. He was just another connection to another country that Salazar wanted ties with.

"Look who finally graces us with their presence," Emilio greeted as my father walked in with Pedro and three more of his men.

My father and I locked eyes for a few seconds before he proceeded on his way. He stood in his place behind Salazar while the other men stood guard by the doors. I could still feel his concentrated stare burning a hole on the side of my face like a ticking fucking grenade. We didn't have any sort of relationship, at least not anymore. We never spoke, leaving so much animosity and unfinished business looming between us. Building up more and more with each passing year, like a raging fire neither one of us could ever extinguish.

I moved into my own apartment a few days following the massacre, after seeing my father for who he really was. He didn't so much as bat an eye about me leaving, as if he expected it or something. It wouldn't even surprise me if he didn't know where I lived.

As far as I was concerned.

Our family died the same day Amira's did.

It didn't take long until Ricardo and his two men walked through the double doors. I watched their every move as they made their way to the table. Ricardo stopped to greet Emilio, while his guards sat in the empty chairs in front of me. Leaving the one between them open for their boss. Emilio stood, embracing him in a hug. Both patting each other's backs, saying it had been too long since they'd seen one another. From an outsider looking in, it appeared as if two old friends were just reuniting and rekindling their friendship.

It was bullshit.

Salazar embraced everyone for two reasons. One, he wanted you to feel like his friend. Unaware that he would slit your fucking throat the second you weren't of use to him any longer. And two, he wanted to feel around your body and mentally count how many guns you were strapped with. He never told me any of this, it was just one of the many things I observed along the way.

The two of them took their seats and spoke about old times for a few minutes, reminiscing about this and that. Trying to portray the meeting for anything but the political corruption that it was. Then they finally got down to fucking business.

"How many kilos in the crates?" Emilio asked.

"As many as you want," Ricardo nonchalantly replied, nodding to him.

"I would say no more than ten kilos and ten crates. That's enough to keep crime going for a few months and the cops busy in Cuba. I want to maintain jobs, not pollute my country."

"Of course, Salazar. I know it's always been about the good of the people with you. I can have those transported over here in no time. I'll get my men on it as soon as I get back. How do you want it shipped over? I can get a private plane with no hassle."

Emilio shook his head. "It's too risky. This isn't the sixties anymore. I have the United States on my ass. They're watching every flight coming in and out of Cuba. They have been for decades. The Yankee pieces of shit won't let us live. My people are starving. There is barely any gas for transportation. With Russia struggling, we have no exchange with them anymore. It's why I've turned to drugs. Need to keep some sort of economy going. Something appealing to get those young Yankee motherfuckers to travel to Cuba. I need tourism most of all. You know how word of mouth spreads. The drugs and pussy are always where the money is at. My girls are the best, now the drugs will be too."

Ricardo nodded, understanding. "I have a few names I can contact in Miami. There are some Feds I know, who I can call in a favor to. I can also reach out to Alejandro Martinez. That son of a bitch knows everyone. It's the least I could do."

"I appreciate that, but now's not the time. Perhaps it would be something to consider in the future. I think it would be safer if we used boat transportation, during the night. The cargo would need to be unloaded no later than five o' clock in the morning on the dock. The crates will need safe transportation until they offload at the port. I'll pay you half now and half when they get delivered."

"No problem. Whatever you want, my friend. I can make it all happen, Emilio. It's not about the money. We're old comrades, I'm here to help you," Ricardo answered, never taking his eyes off Salazar.

And I never took my stare off Ricardo, sizing him up the whole damn time. Unable to hold my tongue any longer, I casually remarked, "You're being awfully cooperative for a man known for the exact opposite. From what I hear, you're nothing but a wolf in sheep's clothing."

"I—"

I put my hand up in the air, silencing him. "That wasn't a question."

"Damien…" Emilio warned in a tone I didn't appreciate.

I grinned, glancing over at him. "How does that saying go? Keep your friends close and your enemies' closer?" Looking back at Ricardo, I continued, "Let's put it to the test, shall we? You've known your old friend Salazar here for quite some time, eh? What did you say it was, Emilio? Forty, forty-five years?"

"Damien, why are you interrogating Ricardo?" Salazar broke in, bringing my attention back to him.

"Just having a friendly conversation with one of your allies. Getting to know him man to man. But just hear me out. It's about to get good."

"Emilio, I think we're done with this meeting. I'll be in touch," Ricardo declared as he stood to leave. His men followed suit.

"Before you haul ass, why don't you tell your old *comrade* what you were up to on July 24th?

He froze mid-stance, completely caught off guard by my question.

I smiled. "Oh, that got your attention." I leaned into the table, cocking my head to the side. "Or better yet, next time you try to come in here with your bullshit cooperation, I suggest you cover your tracks. *Now*, take a seat," I firmly ordered.

His eyes widened, his mind was spinning as he calculated his next move. "You don't know what you're talking about."

I stood up from my chair, and placed my hands in my pockets. Walking to the opposite side of the table. Never once breaking eye contact with him. "I don't? See, I thought we were in the business of making things happen, and the only thing you've made happen is setting up your so called friend."

Ricardo immediately narrowed his eyes at me, taking in my words. "Emilio, I don't know what this piece of shit is insinuating, but I've heard enough. Is this how you run your country now? Allowing your *boys* to run their mouths, disrespecting your guests? I suggest you tell your bitch to back down before I put a bullet in his head."

"No disrespect, Ricardo. I don't know what has come over my soldier, but I will handle it as I see fit," Emilio chimed in, giving me another warning glare. "It was great catching up. Please give my regards to your family."

He nodded to Emilio still trying to hold his ground, even though it was caving beneath him. "Till next time, my friend." With that, he stood, turning his back to us. Ready to leave.

"Ricardo, you didn't answer my question, so allow me to rephrase," I calmly stated, stopping him dead in his tracks. "What exactly were you doing on July 24th at the American Embassy?"

He turned around and in three long strides, he was in my face with his gun pulled. Aiming it right between my eyes. Triggering my father to step in front of Salazar and draw his gun with only Ricardo in his sight.

"Again, motherfucker, I don't know what you're talking about. I was in Puerto Rico, balls deep in my fucking mistress, if you must know," he gritted out, getting up in my face.

I didn't even flinch, unfazed by the cool metal on my forehead. Grinning big and wide, daring him to pull the fucking trigger.

"That's enough!" Emilio roared, his voice echoing off the walls. "Ramón, back the fuck down! Damien, get the hell out of here! I will deal with you later!"

"But the fun just got started," I rasped, stepping back and away from him.

Ricardo didn't waver, redirecting the aim of his gun to my chest. Snidely smiling, thinking he gained the upper hand. I leisurely glanced down, looking at the red laser mark that was now placed over my heart. Grinning as I slowly gazed up through the slits of my eyes. Waiting a few seconds before taking the backs of my fingers and wiping away his target as if it was just a speck of dust.

Mocking him.

"Puerto Rico, eh?" Without any further ado, knowing I got my point across. I reached inside my military jacket, pulling out an envelope from the hidden pocket. "This says otherwise," I argued, throwing it on the table, spilling out the contents. Pictures and documents lined the surface, laying out the truth of Ricardo's betrayal.

"What the fuck is all this?" Emilio asked, narrowing his eyes at me. He grabbed onto the most incriminating piece of evidence. A time-stamped photo of Ricardo shaking hands with the Ambassador at the U.S. Embassy in Colombia.

"A picture is worth a thousand words, and that just spoke volumes," I added, watching as Salazar picked up the document signed by Ricardo, agreeing to help the United States take down Cuban dictator, Emilio Salazar.

"Emilio, I—"

"I've known you over forty-years, and you come into my territory with the intentions of betraying me?"

"It's not what it looks like," he breathed out, lowering his gun like the pussy he was.

"From the looks of that," I chimed in, gesturing to the table filled with the evidence, "you were *balls deep* into plotting his demise."

With one sweep of his arm, Emilio sent all the papers flying to Ricardo's feet. Roaring, "You fucking traitor!"

Ricardo shook his head in disbelief, taking in all the proof he needed, knowing he wasn't getting out of this with any of his bullshit lies. He looked up, meeting Salazar's menacing glare. "Don't take it personal. They came to me! Making me an offer I couldn't refuse."

"What do they know? What did you give them, you miserable fuck?!" Emilio interrogated, stepping around my father.

There was no hesitation as he grabbed ahold of Ricardo and slammed his head onto the table. Lifting him up again, only to deliver another blow to the side of his face, before ramming him to the floor. Ricardo's men pulled out their guns, ready to take out Emilio. Our guards intercepted, breaking both men's arms. Sending them to the ground, reeling in nothing but immediate pain.

"It's your lucky day, motherfucker. I should put a bullet in your head, but I don't want your traitor blood on my hands," Salazar scoffed, spitting in his face. "When everyone finds out about you, your death will be far worse than my fucking bullet." Emilio walked over to me, watching as Ricardo pitifully tried to stand. "You have till the count of three to get the hell out of here. One… two…"

"Fuck this," I coldly interrupted, pulling my gun out from the back of my pants, immediately pulling the trigger. Putting a bullet right between Ricardo's eyes and without giving it a second thought, I targeted his men next.

"Damien, no!" my father yelled as I pulled the trigger once again. Popping another cap into each of their heads.

I shrugged off his order, placing my Glock back into my pants. "There, now their blood is on my hands," I callously stated, walking toward the doors. Not once looking back. Fully aware of what I would see in my father's eyes.

I didn't have the time, nor did I care about anymore of his bullshit lies.

"Ramón, call your men to have this cleaned up. I need to have a word with your son," I overheard Emilio demand from behind me, but I continued on, pushing through the double doors of the warehouse, out to the parking lot.

I was prepared to hear his fucking wrath, conscious of the fact that he was trailing behind me. Most likely wanting to lecture me about my short fuse and temper. How I needed to reel it in, like he always did. I waited, leaning against the hood of my car with my arms folded over my chest. Never expecting what happened next.

"How did you know about Ricardo?" Salazar inquired as soon as we were face to face.

I peered him dead in the eyes and simply answered, "Instinct."

His gaze intensified. An expression I'd never seen before quickly crept across his face. It was only when he followed it up with, "Thank you," that I grasped it as gratitude.

I gave him a curt nod in response, mostly because how the fuck did I reply to that…

"I mean that, Damien. I never pegged Ricardo as a threat. You saved my ass."

"I did what I had to do. Don't make it into something it's not."

"I know you're not happy serving in the military. So here is your one and only chance to back away. What do you want in life? Tell me."

Never in my wildest dreams did I think I would have the option to choose. The answer left my mouth faster than the question left his. "The law. I want to be an attorney."

He smiled, gripping onto my shoulder, with pride and honor radiating off him. "Ahhh… following in my footsteps. I couldn't be prouder, you want to be an attorney like me. After what I just saw, there's not a doubt in my mind that I could use you for far greater things. Consider it done. I'll be in touch with your enrollment and course load." Without another word, he got in his limo and left.

Leaving me there with only my scattered thoughts. I contemplated life for what seemed like the hundredth goddamn time. If it wasn't about Amira, it was about Emilio. Neither one of them were ever far from my mind. Two opposite ends of the spectrum where both of them were completely wreaking havoc on my whole fucked up life. Which once again took another drastic turn in a matter of minutes. I would never say that Amira was a burden, but she also wasn't my choice. Exactly the same way Salazar wasn't one either.

His question, "*What do you want in life*?" echoed in my mind, residing deep into my core. I realized for the first time that I was given a choice, and I didn't hesitate to become like the man who was handing me that option.

I didn't turn into the monster they wanted me to be...

He had always been inside of me.

The doors behind me opened, pulling me away from my thoughts. I didn't have to wonder who it was. I turned, locking eyes with my father.

He took one look at me and asked, "Who are you?" Shaking his head in disappointment, backing away. He didn't even give me a chance to reply, turning around and leaving as if he already knew the answer all along. When it only had just hit me.

That realization alone sent me spiraling down a bottle of fucking bourbon. Before I knew it, I was sitting on a black leather couch, in a dark corner of one of Emilio's whorehouses, out of sight. Not bothering to remove my dark tinted sunglasses. Exhausted from the day and the never-ending plaguing emotions that tortured me every single goddamn day.

I'd come here often to drown my sorrows in bourbon and whores. Typically, after something pivotal happened in my life, or when I needed to unwind. Fuck out my frustrations, my cock buried in whoever wanted a piece of me that night. I took another swig off the bottle, watching as the whole world shut off around me. Even if it was just for an instant, it was a moment I reveled in. Only seeing strobes of colored lights and bodies dancing, and fucking in the dark.

"From the looks of it, you're going to need me tonight," the luscious blonde enticed with her red, pouty dick-sucking lips. Wearing nothing but a tiny G-string and a bra that barely covered any of her assets.

"I just need your lips… on my cock. It would make a pretty picture, don't you think?" I coaxed, leaning back into my chair.

She laughed, swinging her long blonde hair over her shoulder. This was foreplay for her. "I see you're here to break more hearts, Mr. Montero. What's it been, two, three weeks? You know the girls get jealous when you don't pay attention to them. You have your own harem of whores here, your pick of the pussy litter. Now I can see why, it's that pretty boy face that makes women fucking wet when they see you coming… literally. Your reputation precedes you, though." She took it upon herself to straddle my lap. Grinding her pussy on my cock to the beat of the house music. "I may be new, but from what I hear, you fuck like a real man. I'm Lola, by the way."

As soon as those words left her tongue, something Emilio once said to me flashed through my mind. *"I knew your first taste of pussy would teach you to fuck like a real man. Reap the dominance I knew laid dormant in you for so long. Like I told you before, women always love that."*

He wasn't wrong.

Being with Teresa taught me one thing and one thing alone.

Control.

My first time, given the fucked-up situation, didn't end my craving for it. If anything, it made it worse. I thrived on the control as much as I did on anything else. In and out of the bedroom.

It was just who I was now.

I didn't know how to fuck any other way. I had to dominate the sex. Positioning them where I wanted, how I wanted. Dictating the movements of their hips while they rode my cock, hard and fast.

There was no kissing or sleepovers, I fucked them and made them fuck me. The rougher the better. They were ordered to keep their mouths shut, not saying so much as a word without my permission. Call it whatever you want, but it was the only way I could avoid seeing the images of Teresa. Reliving what I was forced to do to her that night, all over again.

It wasn't always about me, though. I'd always make them come, which was probably another reason they wanted me so bad. Not many men cared about a woman's needs. Their minds set on the fact that they were whores for a reason.

Especially men like me.

"I want you," she breathed out, leaning in to kiss me.

I gripped onto her hair at the nook of her neck, tugging her head back, hard. Making her whimper like a dog in fucking heat. She should've known better, I didn't kiss. It was much easier this way. Being with a whore. Don't get me wrong, I never forced another woman sexually.

They wanted it.

Getting pussy had never been an issue. Women literally threw themselves on my dick, as soon as they saw me walking in beside Emilio. Knowing who I was and what I meant to him. Especially the women who wanted a job where the cops wouldn't fuck with them, aware they'd be protected by Emilio's hand. That's how easy it was for them to get on their knees and suck my cock.

This chick wasn't any different.

I let go of her hair and slowly moved my hands from her neck to her ample tits, down to her narrow waist. She licked her lips, sucking in another breath when I suddenly gripped onto her hips. Placing her on the table in front of me so I could get a good fucking look at her.

I stood, spreading her legs to stand in between them. Getting close to her face, I rasped, "What makes you think I care about what you want?" Meaning every last word.

She inhaled, holding her breath as my hand continued its descent, running along her smooth, heated skin, down to her cunt. "Please…"

she begged, looking into my eyes with nothing but need and urgency, so fucking aroused. The tips of my callused fingers awakening every last fiber of her being. Slowly and deliberately, I took my time, knowing damn well I was fucking ruining her for any other man.

"I'm desperate for you," she purred, with nothing but hooded eyes.

I snidely smiled, cocking my head to the side. Taking a second to look into her pleading gray eyes before leaning into her ear, spewing, "Then get on your fucking knees and show me what desperate looks like."

Her eyes instantly dilated as she slowly knelt in front of me, never taking her heady gaze off mine. I immediately reached for my belt buckle, undid my pants, and pulled out my cock in one swift movement. Jerking myself off in front of her face, not giving a flying fuck there were people around us.

She licked her lips, salivating at the size of my cock. I gripped onto the back of her neck this time, crudely tugging her toward me. Causing her to gasp at the sudden shift in my demeanor.

"You trust me?" I baited, and she nodded, not hesitating for one fucking second.

I didn't think twice about it, I took the head of my cock and traced the outline of her red, pouty goddamn lips before shoving it to the back of her throat without any warning. She gagged, choking on my cock. Panting for air that I was savagely taking away from her. I fucked her face. Taking away all my frustrations from the day, exactly how she knew I needed.

I glared down at the luscious blonde with a devious stare, viscously gritting out,

"You shouldn't."

El SANTO

11
Damien

By the time I walked into my apartment, it was just past ten o'clock at night. I had spent the rest of the day fucking every hole of that blonde at the whorehouse. Hoping it would mask all the bullshit taking up occupancy front and center in my mind. I was emotionally, mentally, and physically drained.

It was game fucking over.

At least for tonight.

My feet moved on their own accord out to the balcony that overlooked the ocean. Craving the fresh air, yearning for the tranquility that it usually provided for me. I would spend hours out on the terrace or down at the beach, watching and listening to the soft lull of the waves crashing into the shore. Welcoming the warm, salty breeze coming off the water. It always had a way of calming my nerves no matter what I was feeling or going through, and something told me tonight wouldn't be any fucking different. I slipped off my jacket, laid it over the railing, and rolled up my sleeves. Resting my forearms on the steel bar. Trying to wrap my head around all that had happened in the last thirteen hours, but failing miserably at doing so.

My mind wandered aimlessly as I took in the night's air and the dark sky. Mesmerized by the high-rise buildings that lined the shore, the lights illuminating the streets, and the cars driving by in the distance. Taking in every last detail, needing to come down from the high that killing men and fucking whores always gave me. There was something about the sound of the waves and the ocean breeze that took me away to another place in time. A familiar sense of longing came over me, making me remember how much Amira loved the water.

"Wow! This is your apartment? It's so big for only one person," Amira observed, walking around the living room. It was the first time I brought her over since she started living with Rosarío, seven months ago.

"It's not that big, Muñeca, you're just small."

She placed her hands on her hips with Yuly dangling from her fingers. "I'm not small. You're just abnormally large."

I chuckled, making her smile. I swear this kid's smart-ass mouth was going to be the death of me. As the weeks went by she started to come into her own, crying less and laughing more. She was constantly talking about one thing or another, barely letting me get a word in edgewise. I never imagined a nine-year-old little girl would have so much to say. She had an opinion about everything and wasn't intimidated to speak her mind. It was a nice change of pace to have her around, especially since I was mostly alone before she unexpectedly came barging into my life.

"It's got two bedrooms in the back. In case you ever need to crash. You'll have your own room."

"Why? We can just share a room like we do at Rosarío's."

I touched the end of her nose, and for some reason it always made her eyes light up. "You're not going to be nine forever, Amira. One day it won't be appropriate for us to share a bed anymore, and when that day comes, you'll have your own space in my apartment."

She shrugged, not paying me any mind, walking toward the balcony. "Whatever, I'll just sneak into your room when I have nightmares."

I shook my head, stifling a laugh. "Ay, Muñeca..."

"What?" She turned to look at me. "You know I don't like to sleep by myself, Damien. You keep the monsters away. Plus, I don't

need all those itchy blankets that Rosarío has, you're like a heating blanket. Just lying next to you, I'm nice and warm."

"Amira, you can't say shit like that."

She arched an eyebrow, scratching her head. "I can't say shit like what?"

"Like that," I asserted, pointing at her. "You definitely can't swear. Rosarío will wash your mouth out with soap. Trust me, she tried plenty of times with me."

"Then why do you still use them?"

"Because I'm a man," I simply stated. "You're far too sweet and young to be saying vulgar things. You will be a lady. Don't let me hear you swear again. Do you understand me?"

"Then maybe you shouldn't be teaching me your bad habits." She abruptly spun back around, flipping her long brown hair over her shoulder, and stepped out onto the balcony. "Your apartment overlooks the ocean! I'm never leaving! Do you remember, Damien? How I told you I wanted to have a house like this too? Just like the Little Mermaid!" she excitedly exclaimed, jumping up and down.

I leaned against the glass door, folding my arms over my chest, shaking my head. I couldn't help but be amused by her subtle way of changing the subject. "I remember, Amira." And I did, it was the only reason I got this place. "How about we go for a swim? Rosarío brought over a few bathing suits for you."

She sighed, bowing her head.

"What? What happened?"

"I don't know how to swim."

"Well, lucky for you, I do and can teach you how," I reassured her, extending my hand for her to take. "Come on. You'll be a mermaid in no time."

She smiled again, peering up at me through her long, thick lashes that always reminded me of the dolls I'd buy her.

"And Yuly?" she added, attentively waiting for my reply.

I nodded. "Yes, Muñeca. Yuly too."

As much as I wanted to go see Amira, there wasn't a chance in hell I'd let her witness me like this again tonight. It had been several months since I lost my shit on her at Rosarío's, showing her the man behind the façade. I was worried that night would change her attitude toward me, she would become guarded and possibly frightened to be around me, but she didn't. If anything, she became more attached. Worrying about me in her Amira sort-of-way.

She started leaving me with a bunch of random things, always including Yuly. I'd find them stashed in my car, my jackets, and my overnight bag. Anywhere she knew I'd look later on when she wasn't around. As if she knew I needed to laugh or smile at some point during the day.

It ranged from books with highlighted passages in the chapters, to collected flowers for my apartment, to cookies she baked that tasted like shit, but I still ate them anyway. These were just to name a few. She never bothered asking me about the items. All she knew was I had found them, as soon as Yuly had unexpectedly returned to her room. I would place the doll on her bed when she wasn't looking, or when she was off with Rosarío or by herself in the garden.

For Amira's fourteenth birthday I had her favorite flower, white Mariposas, planted in the backyard with several trellises that lined the side of the house. More Mariposas and vines intertwined, blanketing the soil and spread up the lattice. The garden quickly became her new obsession. She'd spend hours out there with Rosarío or her chickens, pulling weeds and making sure the plants were properly taken care of. She'd prance around with a flower behind her ear as she twirled in circles, flapping her arms like a butterfly, wearing her flowy garden dresses that had rips and stains at the bottom. Probably from being barefoot and running through the grass every chance she got. She was still a ranch girl at heart.

I'd walk into the kitchen and hear her laughter cascading off the greenery from the open sliding doors. The same little girl who used to cry herself to sleep, didn't have a care in the world when she was out there. It was one of the most beautiful things I had ever gotten to see, over and over again. I always took a few seconds to soak up her contagious sounds, smiling to myself, knowing that I had done something right by her. Since the night I lost my temper, I found myself gravitating toward Amira more often than not. It only took a moment of weakness on my behalf for her to witness the side of me that everyone had met. Experiencing my wrath that I spent years shielding her from.

Except, I wasn't a monster in her eyes.

Not even close.

From the second we locked eyes, a sense of protection and possession came over me. It was the craziest thing I had ever felt, but I couldn't help it. It was there, threading itself into my skin, making me feel warmth and contentment. She awakened something within my being, causing me to feel less fucking dead inside. Her energy, her innocence, her love for me, it all became a magnet. Little by little she became a staple piece in my world that I needed in order to keep going.

I may have saved her life.

But she kept me alive.

None of it made any sense. Our connection was solely linked through darkness, but now there was blinding light added into the mix. We were balancing on the tightrope of existence, walking the thin line toward each other, waiting for the inevitable to happen. Not knowing which way we'd fall.

Into the dark or light.

It only seemed like yesterday she was sneaking into my bedroom when she had a nightmare. *"I'm sorry I woke you up again. I know you're really tired," Amira muttered loud enough for me to hear as she turned to face me.*

I'd lost count of how many times she'd woken me up from one of her night terrors. It had become a routine, usually a few hours after she fell asleep. Tonight, we were watching a movie on the couch and she had passed out near the end. I didn't want to move her, knowing that most of the time it was difficult for her to fall asleep in the first place. I laid a blanket over her tiny frame, making sure to leave the table lamp on beside her. I knew she'd be scared if she woke up alone in a dark room in the middle of the night. Amira was comfortable staying in my apartment, but sometimes she would wake up disoriented as hell until she pushed herself out of the haze her nightmares brought on.

It didn't take long until I felt the bed dip beside me, stirring me awake.

"Sleep is overrated." I grinned, winking at her through the soft lighting coming in through the window from the full moon.

"Did your mami rub your back too? When you were little and had nightmares?" she curiously asked, wanting to learn something about me.

Nothing about her question was surprising. It was a running theme with Amira. She was always looking for answers to questions I wouldn't reply to. Not that I could blame her, all she wanted was to get to know me. Which was much easier said than done. So many conflicting emotions emerged through me in a matter of seconds.

I clenched my eyebrows together, deep in thought. I think I stunned us both when I responded with, "I never met my mother."

"Do you miss her?"

My stare never wavered from the textured ceiling, contemplating how to answer her intrusive question. I thought about nothing and everything all at once, wanting to hold back the truth or, quite possibly, what I really wanted to say, before I finally uttered, "You can't miss what you've never had."

She winced, not expecting that reply to fall from my lips. Quite frankly, I was just as shocked by my response, admitting that out loud for the first time ever. I never wanted anyone's fucking pity, especially hers.

I didn't deserve it.

"What about your papi? Did he ever comfort you?"

I turned my head and narrowed my eyes at her through the darkness, trying to analyze what she saw in me. I'd catch myself doing this often, needing to see myself through her eyes, from a different perspective. They were always hopeful, eager, and full of so much fucking life. When her eyes widened, and she faintly smiled, I swear she knew what I was doing. How in the fuck this ten-year-old little girl could interpret my silence was beyond me.

"It's late, Amira. You need your sleep."

She sighed, disappointed by my lack of response. There wasn't a need for her to know about my life. Hers was already tainted enough because of me. The damage was already done, and the last thing I wanted to do was fuck her up even more. I wanted to keep Amira as innocent and pure as humanly possible, for however long I was capable of. It was the least I could do, I owed it to her and her family.

She smiled again, scooting into the side crevice of my body. Wrapping her arm around my torso to rest her head on my chest. She whispered, "Don't worry, Damien. I'll rub your back if you have a bad dream."

I chuckled, kissing the top of her head. Another natural endearment I had always had for her, and I didn't have that for anyone else.

Affection.

"Aye, Muñeca, you have such a big heart. Don't ever change. Not for anyone. Including me."

After that night, she never stopped prying for answers. Except now they weren't in such an elusive way. She no longer tiptoed around the subject like she used to.

About my past.

My present.

My fucking future.

It didn't matter how many times I reverted the questions back to her. Amira wouldn't give up. The first time she saw me, I knew she felt a certain familiarity in my presence. It was the reason she was always so comfortable around me to begin with. As the years continued to go by, it only became more undeniable that the emotion she had perceived was much more than just her safety. There were times when she didn't have to say one fucking word, just being around her brought a sense of calm over me. She knew it too.

And no fucking good could ever come of that.

Specifically, for her.

The pounding knock on the door tore me away from the realm of my purgatory. I had lost all concept of time as soon as I stepped foot out on that balcony, crossing the threshold somewhere between reality and my plaguing thoughts. I took one last swig of bourbon straight from the bottle and shook off my demons. Needing to regain my thick-skinned, fierce composure before I walked back inside. Curious to see who the impatient fuck, incessantly banging on my door, was.

I was shocked as shit when I finally opened it.

"The fuc—"

He shoved past me, barging right in as if he was invited. Fully aware he wasn't even fucking welcome. I couldn't resist breathing out a snide chuckle as I kicked the door shut behind me and leaned against it. I slowly placed my hands in the pockets of my fatigues, cocking my head to the side. Watching the son of a bitch's every move as he made his way around the open floor plan of my apartment, looking for I don't know what.

"So you do know where I live?" I greeted, desperately wanting to get this family fucking reunion over with.

My father abruptly stopped at the kitchen island, intently eyeing me up and down. Time seemed to stand still as his stare gradually made its way back up to my face. From the moment his eyes barred into mine, it started to unravel a deep resolve within my core. While he anxiously searched for any remnants of his long, lost son, with nothing but a reminiscent glare. I could see my childhood flash before his eyes as he stood directly in front of me. Each time he blinked, another milestone from my life came into his sight. All of it. Every memory, every emotion…

The good.

The bad.

The destructive.

Leading us right back to that night as if the last five years didn't exist. Like nothing had changed between us, when in fact, everything had. Every last one of his demons were emerging, clouding the small space amongst us. It all hit him so fucking hard to the point that the walls started caving in on him.

The answers he needed.

The truth he was looking for.

The reality of his mistakes and regrets.

They were all burying him alive, and I would be lying if I said I didn't feel it. But too many lies had come between us, too many dead bodies killed by my own two hands. All in the name of what he instilled in me to do.

I was growing anxious and impatient from the mixture of emotions he stirred inside of me. I hadn't felt them for him in so fucking long. The sentiments dwelled in the dark hollow space of my heart where he used to exist.

You see, I didn't just lose my soul that night…

I lost my father too.

The man who made me was also the man who destroyed me. Condemning us both straight to Hell.

There wasn't an inch of my skin that didn't feel his love or judgmental glare, and I couldn't fathom which one was worse. I could no longer just stand there, having him analyze me as if I was just some goddamn lab rat.

Unable to deal with this sentimental bullshit. I spitefully mocked, "Do you like what you see?" Needing to once again regain the control of my surroundings and emotions.

"No, Damien, I don't. Quite frankly, I don't think you do either. Am I wrong?"

"You're not right," I countered, pushing off the door. "Why don't you cut the bullshit and tell me what the fuck I can do for you?"

"Jesus, son—"

I got right up in his face. "I'm not your son anymore, and I haven't been in a long fucking time."

He grimaced, raising his hands in the air in a surrendering gesture. "I didn't come here to fight with you."

"No? Then why are you here? Just to be a pain in my ass?"

He slowly moved away from me, but I stepped toward him, not backing down. I wasn't playing this cat and mouse game, not in my fucking home. The one I made without him, when I left *his*.

"I didn't want this life for you, Damien," he confessed, as if he could read my mind.

"What life are you referring to exactly? The one you raised me in?"

"That's not fair."

I shook my head, sneering, "You have some balls coming into my home, playing fucking martyr when you're the one who damned me from the start."

"I didn't think Emilio would—"

"You didn't think Emilio would what? See the boy you trained for combat? The same person who you taught to respect and admire everything he stood for? My dominant traits, my controlling mannerisms, my fucking memories of meetings, speeches, and everything in between… Christ, old man. All you did was personally create me for him."

He instantly jerked back like I had hit him, and in a way, I had. Words had the power to cut you far worse than any knife could make you bleed. I had five years of pent-up words to suck him dry.

“Those weren’t my intentions,” he justified, never breaking his intense stare. “I wanted you to have the best education, Damien. Train to go into battle in case you were sent to war. I wanted you to be prepared, knowledgeable, and give you the life I never had! Now, I don’t even know who the fuck you are!”

“Do not raise your fucking voice at me. Ever. I’m not a child,” I gritted through a clenched jaw. My temper looming through the thin patience I had left for him. “This man, the one you say you don’t recognize, is the same man you raised. Don’t you ever look me in the eyes again and fucking deny that.” I saw nothing but the years of betrayal through the rage in my vision.

The air was so thick between us he had to back away from the impact of my words stabbing into his skin.

“What do I have to gain, lying to you? Not a damn thing. I’m here because, regardless of what you believe, I’m still your father and I love you. You’re still my son, Damien. You always will be. Nothing will ever change that, no matter how much you try.”

I didn’t even blink an eye, knowing those words were his weapon of choice that he was trying to use to slice right back into me. They weren’t working. I remained the solid man I had trained to be, unfazed by his doting performance.

“Says the man who took five fucking years to show up at his son’s home and declare that.” I slowly clapped my hands, deviously grinning. “Congratulations, you’re father of the fucking year! Now do me a favor. Get the fuck out!”

His eyes widened and his lips parted. My words finally puncturing a hole deep in his heart, exactly where I wanted them to.

“You have lost all decency!” he roared, stepping in front of me again. “You’re right. You’re not my son! Is that what you want? To be dead to me?”

I didn’t falter. “You’re as dead to me as the puta who abandoned her son. But unlike you, I still fucking respect the woman. At least she left knowing she was destined to be a shitty mother. Too bad I can’t say the same for you!”

My head whooshed back from the sudden blow to my face before I got the last word out. I stumbled to the side, grabbing ahold of the counter, stunned. It took me a few seconds to gather my bearings and realize my father had just backhanded me. I couldn't remember the last time someone got in a good hit. It had been that long.

I glared at him, wiping the blood from the corner of my mouth with the back of my hand. "What the fuck! Touch me again, old man, and I will bury you. I don't give a fuck that you're my blood!"

"See! You're exactly like him! Emilio Salazar's clone! You're nothing but a monster! Do you hear me? A fucking monster!" he seethed, his hands rolling into fists at his sides.

The rest played out in slow motion like a bad dream. My father took a step in my direction as the door to my apartment burst open, slamming against the wall. Knocking frames over, sending shards of glass skidding across the floor by our feet.

"No, he's not! You are!"

I never expected who was standing there ready for battle, instantly coming to my defense. Almost knocking me on my ass. I should've known better, but once again…

I didn't.

I never did when it came to her.

12

Amira

I stood there frozen, immediately realizing what I had just done. Revealing my identity that Damien worked so hard to keep off the radar, and possibly endangering both of our lives. I recognized the older man instantly. He was the one who took part in brutally beating my papi that night five years ago. His face still haunted my nightmares to this day. Except, now I knew who he was—Damien's father. I could now see the familiarity in their eyes. The same eyes that held all my savior's truths. He recognized me instantly, the shock evident on his face. He kept looking at me like he had just seen a ghost.

He stepped toward me, his hand extended as if he was going to touch my face to make sure I was real. "You are—"

Damien suddenly appeared out of thin air, crudely shoving his father away from me as hard as he could. Shielding my body behind his. "Don't even think about it, motherfucker. Don't try me," he threatened, holding his hand out in front of him. His warning was loud and clear.

My eyes widened and I swallowed the lump in my throat, witnessing yet another side of the man I thought I knew, for the first time ever. There was something predatory about the way he was guarding me with one arm wrapped around my torso, and his hand steady on the side of my stomach. It reminded me of a lion ready to attack its prey.

"Damien, it's okay—"

"Don't you say one fucking word, not one," he interrupted me in a calm tone, although his demeanor was anything but.

I didn't know what was worse—seeing his vicious fury like the last time, or witnessing this completely opposite side to him that was eerily calm. At least with his rage I knew what I was getting.

His father slowly took a few more steps back toward the front entrance, not taking his troubled stare off mine. "What did you do, Damien? What the fuck did you do?"

"It's none of your goddamn business, now leave and keep your fucking mouth shut. Or I'll do it for you."

He slammed the door shut with no intentions of leaving. "Jesus Christ, do you have any idea what will happen to you both if Emilio finds out you betrayed him?"

"He's not going to find out, now is he?" Damien firmly stated, even though it came out as a question.

"How could you not tell me? Where has she been staying? After all this time… I thought… I thought you had murdered a child."

Unable to control my mouth, I blurted, "You obviously don't know your son! Damien would never do that! He has done nothing but take care of me like I was his own flesh and blood. He's not a murderer like you!"

Damien didn't reprimand me like I thought he would. Instead, he locked eyes with his father, who took one look at me and then back at him. He narrowed his eyes, cocking his head to the side as if he was silently asking him a question. I glanced back and forth between them, trying to figure out the answer, but it was no use.

"You can't promise this girl protection forever. What's going to happen if Emilio sends you somewhere else? Huh? To another city or worse, another country on the other side of the world? Who's going to take care of her then? What about your future wife? Your kids? Do you have any idea the life she's going to have without you?"

I jerked back, never considering any of those questions. We'd been living in our own little world, where I thought we'd stay forever. Not once thinking that reality could rip that away from me. Again. I looked over at Damien to find shelter in his gaze like I had done so many times before. His eyes remained neutral. There was absolutely no change in his composure, making me wonder if he had already considered all those questions.

"Unlike you, old man. I protect what's fucking mine. Nothing is going to happen to her and if someone—anyone—so much as tries," Damien forewarned, pulling his gun out from the back of his fatigues and aimed it at his father's heart. "I won't hesitate to pull the fucking trigger," he paused, letting his words sink in. "Are we clear?"

My stomach was in knots, churning with each tick of the clock. I knew Damien carried several guns, he was never secretive about his weapons. But I had hoped I'd never see him pointing one at another human being again. Especially his own flesh and blood.

His father nodded, eyeing me. Feeling my anxiety radiating off my skin.

"Let me hear you say the words, *Dad*," Damien ordered, never taking his eyes off the man in front of him. Even though I knew he felt my anxiousness too. "I won't ask again."

His hand never left the side of my stomach. His calloused thumb strummed up and down on my exposed skin from where my tank top was rising up, leaving goose bumps in its wake. Igniting a foreign feeling deep in my core and a shiver to run down my spine, but just as fast as it came, it was gone. As if he realized what he was doing and stopped.

At first, I thought it was to ease my worry, providing any comfort he could.

Though now, I wasn't so sure.

"I would never sell you out," he simply replied. "You can trust me, I'm your father."

"I trust no one. Especially you." Damien nodded toward the door, lowering his gun. "We're done here."

There wasn't anything left to say that hadn't already been said. I heard it all through the door before making my grand entrance and most likely the worst mistake of my life.

Finally, his father just backed away, shook his head, and left. Calmly shutting the door behind him. Damien's hand lingered at my side for a few more seconds until he removed it completely. Taking his warmth and affection with him.

"Damien, I'm sor—"

He snapped, "Not right now, Amira," locking the door before walking down the hallway toward his bedroom.

I instinctively followed him, feeling as though he needed me. "Can you just let me expla—"

He whipped around, stopping inches from my face. His warm, alcohol-infused breath assaulted my senses with a sweet smell that had a spicy kick. Making my stomach flutter. I couldn't give it a second thought because with one look, he rendered me speechless. "I. Said. Not. Right. Now. Amira."

I warily nodded, feeling so guilty and confused. Trying my hardest to keep my tears at bay. The last thing I wanted was for him to see me cry. I couldn't control all the emotions hitting me all at once, the unanswered *what ifs,* spinning around my head. I was beyond overwhelmed with everything that had just went down, scared of what was going to happen with Damien.

With me.

With us.

My family.

"Just be a good girl and go watch television in the living room. Stay inside and out of trouble. I need a minute to myself. You think you could do that?" he added, making me feel worse.

I nodded in agreement. Afraid if I spoke my voice would betray me. Pissing him off even further. He was desperately trying not to lose his temper on me again, except this time I wanted him to. I realized right then and there that I'd take his anger over his silence, any day. I watched him turn his back on me and stalk toward his room, closing his door behind him. It took everything inside of me not to run to him. He had been my only stability for so many years, that I had forgotten what it was like to stand on my own and not have the refuge he always provided for me.

I laid on the couch, listening to the shower run from his master bathroom as I gazed out the balcony doors. Hoping the sound of running water and the serenity of the night's sky would ease my unsettled mind. My eyes started fluttering closed and the next thing I knew, I must have passed out.

"Amira, run faster! You're so slow!" Teresa shouted, running in front of me.

"I am! I am, Teresa! But you're too fast! I can't catch up! Slow down!" I yelled back, trying to get to her.

"I'm not going to slow down, you slowpoke! Come on!" she laughed, about to run into our house.

I saw them before she did.

The monsters.

"NO! Teresa! Don't run in there! Please, don't run in there! They're in there! I can see them! Please!" I pleaded from a distance.

My voice sounded so far, yet so close at the same time. It echoed all around me, making it difficult to tell if she heard me or not. I blinked and was back in the cabinet when I was nine-years-old, except this time everyone could see where I was hiding. They were all staring in my direction.

My family's arms were reaching out for me while the monsters just stood there and laughed.

"Come on, Amira. Don't hide like you did before. Come be with your family. We miss you," Teresa whispered in an eerie tone.

Her voice echoed again, but I couldn't make out where it was coming from. Humming through the house, vibrating deep into my bones. Feeling as if it was now a part of me.

"I want to be with you! I do! I'm sorry! I won't hide!"

"You're the reason they're all dead," the monster roared, his face morphing into my papi's. Then transforming into a pair of familiar eye's that I knew all too well. Except they weren't Damien's, they were his dad's. Barring into mine like they had this evening.

I franticly shook my head, silently praying it would make them go away. Immediately feeling guilty for everything past and present.

"What? I did what you said!" I shouted with tears in my eyes. Raking my hands through my hair as I breathed out profusely. Unable to control any of my emotions from what was happening in front of me.

I blinked again and they all started walking toward me, only now they were covered in blood. It was pouring out of the holes in their heads, soaking every inch of their skin. My hands instantly covered my mouth so I wouldn't scream.

I was terrified.

But at the same time, I was grateful they were there with me.

I never wanted them to go.

I didn't want them to die.

When I glanced down at my hands, their blood was all over my skin.

"Damien? Where are you, Damien? He can save you this time! I know he can! Damien! Damien! Please help them!" I yelled, panic taking over. Trying to wipe their blood off my hands, but it was no use. The more I tried, the more it spread down my arms, my legs.

My whole body.

"Amira, it's time you come with us," Mami said, getting closer and closer to me. The face morphing back and forth, from her to the monster to Damien's father once again. I couldn't tell them apart anymore. "Come to Hell with us. It's where you belong!"

"No! No! No!" My body fervently shook with each word that escaped my mouth. "I don't want to go there! I'm a good person! I hid! I did what Papi told me to do!" I shouted, immediately grabbing

onto my neck. My voice made no sound. I was moving my lips and nothing came out.

I screamed and screamed and screamed.

I screamed until my throat felt raw and my chest burned. While my heart pounded against my ribs, in my ears, and through my mind.

"Amira, Amira, Amira, you're going to Hell with us," they chanted, getting closer to me.

"Please! I'm sorry! I'm sorry! Please! Please! I don't want to go there!" I begged even though they couldn't hear me.

No one could hear me.

I tightly closed my eyes, placing my bloody hands over my ears. Hiding my face into my knees.

I couldn't breathe.

"Shhh… Muñeca. I'm here. Shhh… It's okay, I'm here," I heard Damien's voice soothe in a gentle lull.

The next thing I knew I felt a strong hand start rubbing my back.

"It's okay, I'm here. Shh…" I heard him say, repeating all the same words for I don't know how long.

I followed the sound of his voice, the movement of his hand, placing gentle strokes up and down my back. Pushing everything else away.

The darkness.

My fears.

"Shhh… Muñeca. Shhh… I'm here. It's okay, I'm here."

Then, all of a sudden, the monsters were gone.

And there was nothing left but peace.

When I stirred awake, Damien was on the floor in front of the couch, using one arm to prop his head up on the cushion, and the other was still rubbing my back.

"It's been a while since you had a nightmare, Muñeca. In fact, it's been months," he stated, purposely staring out the balcony doors as I was before I fell asleep. The full moon dimly lit the living room, casting shadows of darkness on his face. Producing enough light so I could see his tormented expression. The one I always tried so hard to push away.

"It's nothing," I replied, aware he was lost in his thoughts. Only fueling the remorse and shame I knew he was once again reliving.

"It didn't sound like nothing."

I took a deep breath, inhaling the mixture of his masculine scent and musky cologne that surrounded me. Giving me the confidence I needed to initiate this conversation with him. It resided deep in my pores, consuming my attention as he hovered next to me. Bringing back the same sense of comfort and familiarity that it always provided, alongside his secure presence. His long, wet hair had fallen around his face, framing it perfectly. Accentuating the intensity of his honey-colored eyes, although this time it was solely his regrets that were pouring out of them.

I took a steady, reassuring breath, whispering, "What happened to my family, to my sister… it wasn't your fault."

He didn't attempt to move away.

He didn't look at me.

He didn't even stop rubbing my back.

It wasn't until I said, "You were a victim that night as much as I was," that he suddenly stood up and made his way out the sliding door, onto the balcony.

The second I stepped over the threshold, standing behind him, he revealed, "You're a child. I could tell you a fucking fairy tale and you'd believe me. Guilt and fault are foreign feelings to a little girl. You don't know what you're talking about. Don't make me out to be something I'm not. I'm far from a fucking victim. You don't know me, Amira. If you did, you wouldn't be here right now."

"That's bullshit, and you know it," I honestly expressed, cussing at him for the first time. Needing to get my point across.

He turned around, leaning his back against the railing. Crossing his arms over his fit chest with a stern look on his face.

"Oh! So that's what gets a reaction. I need to start swearing more often."

"Don't test me, Amira. Trust me, you won't like the outcome."

I had the sudden desire to mock his uptight words in that moment, just to have him follow through with that threat. Wanting to feel his touch that was home to me. But I decided now wasn't the time. I shook it off, earning a small grin to escape from his lips. He knew what I was thinking. It persuaded me to continue on.

"I don't care what you claim. I know you, Damien. I may not know what you do every day, but who cares. I don't even know what Mama Rosa does every day. That doesn't mean I know her any less than I know you. I may be young, but I'm not a child. I'll be fifteen in less than six months. That probably sounds like a kid to you, but that's just because you're old," I teased, knowing it would get a rise out of him. He was only twenty-three.

He scoffed out a chuckle.

"I know the man that you are in here." I placed my palm over his heart. "The guy you are when you're with me, and that's all that's ever mattered and that's the reality of our friendship. So please stop pushing me away. I'm not scared of you, Damien. I never have been. I'm definitely not going to start shying away from you now."

"Why are you here, Muñeca?" he asked out of nowhere, changing the subject. Removing my hand from his chest. I would be lying if I said it didn't hurt my feelings he was rejecting my touch.

"I was worried about you." I shrugged. "You always tell me when you can't come over to Mama Rosa's and… I just wanted to make sure nothing had happened to you. That's all."

"So you thought sneaking out and coming to my apartment in the middle of the night. Alone. Would do what, exactly? Bring me happiness?"

"Well, when you put it that way, no. I don't really like the way you're being with me right now, though."

"Do you think it makes a difference to me, if you like it or not? I can't imagine you'd think I'd let this slide."

"Is it because I snuck out? Or because I eavesdropped? Or simply because I defended you, revealing to your dad I was still alive?"

"All of the above, Amira. Do I look like I need your protection? You're just a little girl."

"No! I think you need my love. My concern for you. I mean, somebody has to take care of you too. Mama Rosa has tried, but I'm way younger and capable, so… it's my turn." I smiled, stepping toward him until we were standing inches apart, looking up into his face. "In my defense, we've never talked about that horrific night, and I've spent the last five years trying to forget it. I remember you going off on Rosarío the same night, but so much was being discussed between the two of you that it was hard to keep up. I didn't realize your father was one of the men…" I hesitated, wanting to choose my words wisely. "I'm just trying to explain to you that I would've never barged in like that if I would've known that he was one of them. I'm sorry, Damien. I didn't mean to ruin everything you've sacrificed for me."

"The damage is already done. There is no use in apologizing for things that can't be changed."

"Is that why you don't like to talk about your family or your past? Because of what your father did to my—"

"It's late, Amira, you need to go to bed."

I frowned, not hiding my disappointment. I thought for once I was getting through to him. He was finally letting me in, only to slam me down once again.

"Can I sleep in your room with yo—"

"No."

I bowed my head, sighing, "Okay." But then he touched the end of my nose with his index finger, causing me to look up at him through my lashes.

"We can sleep on the couches. If you need me, I'll still be there."

I smiled as he nodded toward the living room for us to go inside, and right as I turned to go back in, I changed my mind at the last second. I spun back around, hugging him as tight as I could instead. "Please, don't be mad at me. You've never been mad at me before, and I really don't like it. I'm really sorry. All I want is for you to be safe. You and Mama Rosa are all I have. I wouldn't know what to do if I lost you too. I love you, Damien. You're my family."

He let out a heavy sigh, wrapping his arm around my torso, kissing the top of my head. I held in the tears that threatened at the surface, listening to his heart beating steadily against my cheek. I couldn't understand why I was being so overly emotional tonight. Maybe it was because I hated the feeling of disappointing him, knowing so many others had done the same.

I wanted to be different…

I needed to be different.

For him.

"I know, Muñeca. I know…"

And I knew in my heart.

He did.

13
Damien

"You better not be fucking me over. This is a life or death situation," I stated over the phone, walking toward the dock.

"You have my word," he replied.

"Your word means shit to me."

"My word is all I have. I don't fuck with women or kids, and I have no desire to start now."

"So the devil does have a heart?"

Completely ignoring my statement, he continued on, "Alvaro will be wearing a white shirt, jeans, a ball cap, and a fucking smile. He will also have a newspaper in his hand. I'll be in touch."

"Wait!" I stressed, knowing he was about to hang up. "I just wanted to say thank you… for everything."

"Don't thank me yet. She's still not in the clear." With that, he hung up.

I placed my cell phone in my back pocket, arriving at Ciudad Mar dock. Searching for the man who he had just described seconds ago. It didn't take long to spot him on the pier. He was leaning against a tie-up post, actually reading the fucking newspaper.

"Alvaro, I presume?"

Peering over the paper, he nodded. Eyeing me up and down, taking in my appearance. "Yeah. I didn't catch your name?"

"No shit. I didn't give it out. You don't need to know who I am." I did a quick sweep of the perimeter with my eyes. Checking our surroundings before reaching into my jacket and pulling out an envelope full of hundred-dollar bills. "My money will speak for itself." I handed it over to him.

He looked inside, smirking. "Don't need to count it, right? You look like you're good for fifteen grand or more."

"You can wipe your ass with it for all I care. I just need to know when and where the drop off is?" I resisted the urge to wipe the smug expression off his face.

"You're looking at it. Be back here tonight at midnight."

I nodded and left. There was no need for pleasantries. He was a means to an end. Besides, it was Amira's fifteenth birthday, and I was already running behind. I tried not to think about anything on the drive over to Rosarío's, but that was easier said than done. My mind was fucking spiraling out of control, more so than usual these last six months. The one thing I didn't want to dwell on was the only thing that wouldn't go the fuck away.

"Tell me, how are your law classes going?" Emilio inquired from behind his desk.

"The same as last week when you asked."

"You've been in college for quite a few months now. Your grades from the spring semester have you at the top of your class. Not to mention the double course load you're taking. I'm surprised you can even sleep, let alone fuck."

I chuckled, "Priorities, I do what I can."

He leaned back into his leather chair, propping his boots up on his desk, getting comfortable. "I always told your father, Rosarío was spoiling you. I can only imagine how much she is now that you're a full-time student. How is the old bat by the way?"

His eyes glazed over. It was quick, but I saw it. This wasn't one of our usual conversations. He was subtly interrogating me. Looking for I don't know what.

"She is the same as she's always been," I casually retorted, not missing a beat.

"You know I stopped by the other day, but no one was home."

He was so full of shit. Salazar wouldn't dare walk into Rosarío's modest home. In fact, he didn't even know where she resided, now that she no longer lived with my father. Rosarío fucking hated him, avoiding him at all costs. He knew it too. He was reaching, trying to make me slip up.

"That's a shame, she would have loved seeing you." I played along, not giving him a fucking inch. Making sure to keep steady eye contact with the man I used to admire. When people lied, their eyes shifted or they blinked. No civilian would ever notice that.

Well, except Emilio or myself.

The horn honking in front of my car brought me back to the present. That was the last time Salazar questioned me about Rosarío, two months ago. Between my father knowing about Amira and Emilio sniffing around, I knew I was making the right choice. Even though it might kill me to have to do it. I made it over to Rosarío's a few minutes later, cursing myself for being so late. I grabbed the small pink gift bag off the passenger seat and walked right inside, not bothering to knock anymore. The music and laughter grew louder and sharper with every step I took toward the back of the house. Knowing exactly where I'd find Amira.

In her garden.

I stepped outside unnoticed, taking a minute to admire the vision in front of me from a distance. I could tell she was wearing one of her long garden dresses, from the rips and stains at the bottom. Her brown hair was cascading all around her face and down to her lower back. It was the first time I noticed how long it was getting. She was spinning around in circles with her arms catching the wind and the sun reflecting off her soft skin. Her eyes were closed and her smile lit up the entire backyard. She looked like a fucking angel, leaving me breathless. I had to lean against the sliding door to gather my bearings. It physically pained me to look at her in that moment, in a way it never had before. I wanted to soak in every last smile, every last laugh, and every last inch of her fucking skin before it was too late.

I shut my eyes, taking a few deep breaths. Needing to reel in the emotions coursing through my veins, or I wouldn't be able to go through with this. Knowing what I had to do was fucking killing me. I counted to three to stabilize my pounding heart that throbbed mercilessly against my ribs. Having to count a few more numbers until I finally found the strength from within to open my eyes, only to unexpectedly meet hers. I wasn't prepared to have her look at me with so much love and devotion that I swear almost brought me to my goddamn knees.

"Damien, are you alr—"

I pushed off the slider to walk over to her. Lifting her off the ground and spinning her around in a circle, making her laugh even louder before I placed her back down on the grass. "Happy birthday, Muñeca," I rasped, pulling her back into a tender hug, needing extra time to hold my life between my arms.

Her body immediately melted into mine, molding perfectly against my chest. I always knew Amira was tiny compared to me, but for some reason she felt even smaller as I held her so close to my heart. Kissing the top of her head, I let my lips linger a bit longer. Wanting to remember her just this way. I was the first to pull away. Aware that if I didn't, I wouldn't be able to let her go.

Ever.

"Hey," I breathed out, touching the end of her nose to gaze into her glossy eyes. "It's your birthday. No crying."

She smiled, nodding. "I know. It's just… the only time I've ever seen that look on your face was the night I met you."

I shoved my nails into the palm of my hand as hard as I could, determined to remain the unaffected man she always knew.

"And then the way you hugged me. It was like you didn't want to let me go." The distress in her voice was as evident as the agony in mine. "Is everything alright? Did your father tell—"

"No." She was always so fucking perceptive. I had yet to figure out if that was just with me or with everyone. "Amira, I told you since day one. You let me worry about everything. Nothing is going to happen to you. I made sure of it."

"What do you—"

"You win, birthday girl. I'm just a little choked up that you're fifteen-years-old today, that's all," I misled, slightly smiling to detour her afflicting thoughts.

It was partially true. I couldn't fucking fathom how fast the years went by. The little girl I saved turned into a young lady, and it was impossible not to be proud of the woman she was becoming.

Amira was the only thing I ever did right.

She smiled wide, it was working. "What? You never get emotional about my birthday. Is it because I'm turning into such a beautiful girl?" She batted her lashes at me.

"Now, you're just fishing for compliments, but I'll take the bait. You've always been beautiful, Muñeca."

She shyly smiled, and her cheeks blushed. It was the first time I'd ever seen that beam in her eyes, and I recognized it all too fucking well. Without saying another word, she got on the tips of her toes, leaned forward and kissed my cheek. A little too close to my mouth. Amira was never timid, she openly showed me affection, though this was different.

For both of us.

She slowly backed away. "Is that for me?" Eyeing her gift that was still in my grasp.

I nodded, handing it over to her. She made it a point to lightly touch the ends of my fingertips as she took it out of my hand. Further proving that I was doing the right thing by her, which was all I wanted.

"Damien…" she muttered, loud enough for me to hear. Smiling from ear to ear when she saw the passport holder I bought her. "It's perfect! Now I can travel the world in style. Thank you!" She kissed my cheek again, but this time it was an innocent gesture. Unlike before.

"Your birthday's not over yet. Go throw on some warm clothes, I have somewhere I want to take you."

She happily listened, prancing into the house so high on life. Yelling over her shoulder on the way to her room, saying something about leaving Rosarío a note, who had to run over to the neighbor's house or some shit. It seemed like all I did was blink and we were in my car almost reaching our destination. Amira was talking about one thing or another as I stared blankly out the windshield, nodding my head every few minutes as if I was paying any attention to what she was actually saying. As much as I wanted to be living in the moment with her, my mind was somewhere else completely. To the point I began to wonder if I would ever fucking think about anything else again.

"We're at Ciudad Mar! I knew you were taking me to the beach. And you've picked one I've never been to! You always give me the best birthdays, Damien! How do you do that?"

"Because I know you," I stated, parking the car. Silently praying I could get through the next few hours without losing my shit.

I grabbed the blanket from the backseat and wrapped it around her shoulders to walk down to the water. Arriving just as the sun was setting over the horizon. I found us a secluded spot near a fire pit in the sand, igniting the wood to keep her warm. Cuban nights were starting to get a little breezy, especially when you were near the ocean. She stared out at the water, aimlessly discussing all the cities she wanted to travel to. How many stamps she'd have in her passport, convinced that one day we'd get out of Cuba, and I would finally show her all the places she wanted to see.

I just sat there next to her, listening intently. Drowning out everything else spinning a web in my fucked-up mind. I couldn't help but stare at the side of her face through the flames and the sparks, soaring up into the dark sky. Seeing the little girl that once wreaked havoc on my life, knowing now she was anything but that any longer.

"Can I lay my head on your legs? I want to look up at the stars and show you something," she coaxed, looking back at me.

"Since when do you ask to lay on me?"

She giggled, shrugging her shoulders. It was still one of the sweetest fucking sounds I'd ever heard. I leaned back, stretching out my legs. Patting my thigh for her to come rest her head on me. She crawled over, lying down immediately.

"Okay, give me a second. I need to find them." She narrowed her eyes, sucking in her bottom lip. Something she did when she was deep in thought. "Alright, found them," she exclaimed, pointing toward a cluster of stars, trying to connect the dots with her index finger so I could follow. "That's Princess Andromeda and that's her husband, Perseus. Do you see how they unite in the middle? You can't tell where one star ends and the other begins, kind of like they're holding hands."

I nodded, waiting to see where she was going with this.

"After consulting an oracle, the King and Queen chained Princess Andromeda to a rock, in order to be sacrificed to the monster."

I grinned and she did too.

"But the hero, Perseus, was nearby and heard of the imminent death of Andromeda. He came to her rescue and saved her from the monster. She returned to Greece and they got married, having nine kids. After Princess Andromeda died, the Goddess of love, Athena, placed her in the sky as a constellation, nearby her beloved husband Perseus. They were two soul mates who were destined to be together forever, so she made them constellations so they would be."

"Where did you learn that?"

"Charo, she's teaching me Greek Mythology."

"And what about that legend made you want to tell me their story?"

She shrugged. "I don't know."

"Yes, you do."

We locked eyes.

"I need you to promise me something," I addressed in a serious tone, unable to hold back any longer.

We needed to get going, but that wasn't the only reason. Her fucking story. There was a similarity to it, almost like it had been written for us.

The princess.

The hero.

The monster…

It was just too much to take. I wasn't a fucking idiot, these last few months Amira had started to find ways to touch me, or to have my hands on her. Excessively teasing me, conscious of the fact that I would tickle her. Not to mention the not-so-subtle ways of making me lay with her at night because she was scared of her dreams. When I knew damn well there weren't any currently haunting her. Just so I'd rub her back. The random items she'd leave me became more personal. She continually started showing up more and more at my apartment unannounced, with some bullshit excuse I never believed.

More needs.

More wants.

More… more… more…

I quickly realized after hearing that story, how deep Amira's feelings had turned for me. It was something I had to put an end to, now.

"Okay…"

"I mean it, Muñeca. In all these years, I've never asked you for a damn thing, but I need you to do something for me."

She sat up, never taking her eyes off mine. "You're scaring me."

"I need you to trust me when I say that everything is going to be alright."

"Damien, what's—"

"Promise me!" I ordered in a rough, demanding voice.

She jerked back, shaking her head. "No. Not until you tell me why."

"Goddamn it, Amira!" I roared, abruptly standing up. "Why can't you ever just do what you're fucking told?"

She followed suit, getting right in my face. "Stop it! Don't do that. Don't turn on me. Just tell me what's going on."

"I'm going to do more than tell you. Let's go." I turned and left before she could reply.

The entire walk toward the dock, I could feel her anxiety searing its way into my skin. Leaving scars that would never fucking heal. She followed closely behind as if she needed to feel the warmth radiating of my back. Giving her a false sense of security. We stopped just under the pier sign, where I had just been standing six hours ago. The loud rev of an engine sounded in the distance, getting closer and closer.

From the second the speedboat came into our sight, I knew I was fucked.

Right when I heard her loudly gasp, "No…"

14

Damien

I simultaneously spun around, ready to grab her and throw her over my fucking shoulder if she tried to run. Her terrified gaze went from the boat, to me, back to the boat, so many fucking times I could barely keep up. She couldn't decide what she wanted to look at more.

The boat that was going to take her away.

Or the man who was making her leave on it.

"Muñeca—"

"Please don't do this," she bellowed, her eyes welling up with fresh tears. "Please, Damien, I'm begging you. Please don't do this." She sounded like the panicked little girl I first met almost six years ago.

Breaking my fucking dark, soulless heart.

"I promise I will listen to everything you say and order me to do. I swear I'll stop teasing you. I'll stop waking you up in the middle of the night. I will do whatever it takes to make you not send me away," she pleaded, her voice breaking profusely. Gasping for her next breath.

I was surprised she managed to get it all out. Tears escaped her eyes, falling down the sides of her shattered face. Fueling the war between what was right and what was wrong. My heart battling my mind, when all I wanted to do was protect her.

"Jesus Christ, Amira. That has nothing to do with it."

"Then why? Why are you doing this? Is it because your father knows about me? He's not going to tell. And if he did, it doesn't matter. I'll hide! That's what I'm good at, you said it yourself! I won't leave the house. I'll stay in my room. I don't care!"

"What kind of life would that be for you?"

"One that's with you! And Rosarío! The only life I know!"

Her words were like taking bullet after bullet to my motherfucking heart. Inflicting pain, far worse than I have ever experienced before. I had to push through. I had to stay strong, this wasn't about me.

It was about Amira.

I needed to get her the fuck out of Cuba.

Right. Fucking. Now.

I stepped toward her, touching the end of her nose causing her to grimace. For the first time the sentiment I had been doing for years, tormented and agonized us both in different ways. I placed my hand on her cheek, hoping she wouldn't recoil away again. I knew what I was about to tell her was going to break her.

"Listen to me. I need you to listen to what I have to say because regardless, Muñeca, I'm placing you on that fucking boat with or without your consent. Do you understand me?"

And she did. She broke. Her chest heaved, her body shook under my touch, and so many goddamn tears fell in between us. I could no longer see her bright, big brown eyes.

"I'm not making you go away, Amira. I'm just following through on my promise to always keep you safe, no matter what. It's not safe for you here anymore. It never has been. If anything were to happen to you, because of me…" I didn't have to continue with what I had to say.

She knew it as much as I did.

"No one's safe here! Especially not you, and if that's the case then you have to come with me. As long as Emilio is alive, you're in danger too. Please Damien! I can't do this without you! I can't live without you!" she repeated until it made itself home within my core.

Where it would eternally live alongside the hatred I already had for myself for everything I had cost her.

I wasn't the least bit shocked at the words falling from her quivering lips. Quite frankly, I was expecting it. I was more shocked it took her that long to say it. I figured it would've been one of the first things out of her mouth.

"I can't go with you," I simply stated, softly caressing her cheek with my thumb. Needing to feel her skin against my callused fingers, even if it was only for a second. I needed her, and that was the only way I could have her. She leaned into my embrace. "I can't protect you anymore, not as long as you are under my care. I'm sorry. I'm so fucking sorry. But my life is here. Without you."

"Well, my life is *with* you, Damien. We could start over. Where no one knows who we are. We could be whoever we want to be. No pasts, no secrets. A real life… together."

Every single word she said went in one ear and out the other. As tempting as it may have sounded, there wasn't a chance in hell I could give her what she wanted. Needed. Not in this life, even though it was the world I always wanted.

"It's time for you to go."

She frowned, bowing her head in defeat. Feeling as though I was doing nothing but rejecting her. Which couldn't have been further from the truth. My hand trembled from her shuddering so fucking hard, at least that's what I told myself.

"Where? Where am I going to go?"

"The speedboat is going to transport you to the straits of Key West, Florida. There will be a black van waiting only for you, ready to take you to Miami. It's going to safely get you to a church where there's a loving family waiting to take you in. They have a nice house, two kids, a fucking dog. All your expenses will be taken care of. I have set up a plan to send money to the family, Amira. You will never want for anything, I promise you. This will be the life you deserve." I grabbed her chin, making her look at me. "One that I will never be able to offer you."

"Oh my god, you don't know me at all, do you? I couldn't care less about any of that shit." She shoved me away.

I grabbed her wrists, tugging her to my body. Pulling her into my arms and holding her tiny frame so fucking tight. Needing to feel something, anything other than what I was fucking feeling. She buried her head into my chest, wrapping her arms around me as tight as she could. Yearning for the same exact thing.

I kissed the top of her head, breathing out, "I'm sorry, Amira, but I do."

She began to hyperventilate, weakly attempting to pound her fists into me. All while breaking down, sobbing uncontrollably. Losing herself to misery. I let her. I deserved it.

Her pain.

Her tears.

Her feeling of betrayal.

"Why? Why, are you doing this? I know you want me, Damien." She shoved her hands into my chest as hard as she could. "Why are you pushing me away? This isn't fair! Not to me, not you, not anyone!" Another two blows, ramming me back. "Why are you just standing here? Say something, goddamn it! I deserve an explanation! I deserve a choice!" She raised her hand to slap me across the face, but I intercepted. Holding her securely in place in front of me. "You're a coward! That's all you are! Admit it! You're scared. You're scared to show any weakness! So I'm getting the brunt of the punishment! Why?" She started to sink to the ground, her leg's giving up on her, much like I was. "Mama Rosa doesn't want me to go, I know she doesn't want me to go…"

"No, Amira, she doesn't know," I told her the truth, she didn't. Rosarío would've never let me go through with this, but in the long run she would understand.

I held her up, welcoming every blow she continued to deliver both physically and mentally. It took everything inside me not to give in, knowing that once she was gone, my world would turn to pitch fucking black. I always thought she was the only light in my life and she was, it was only then that I recognized she was also the darkness.

Amira held the power of both.

Which was probably why our connection had always been so fucking strong. It was brought on by darkness. I gravely wanted to tell her I loved her, knowing exactly how much she needed to hear it.

I couldn't.

I wasn't contrived like that. It only would've made things worse for the both of us.

So I held on to her until I couldn't hold her any longer. The second I tried to pull away, she held me tighter never wanting to let me go.

"Muñeca, please…" I urged in a voice I didn't recognize.

She peered up at me with tears streaming down her beautiful, sunken face. "I can't do this. I can't say goodbye to you. My heart is filled with so much pain," she choked out, trying to suck in air that couldn't be found. "I can't breathe, Damien. I feel like I can't breathe."

I held her face between my hands, and it was like looking into her nine-year-old eyes all over again. Her lips trembled with each second that passed between us. Not once did her gaze leave mine.

Hoping.

Praying.

Waiting.

For me to change my mind.

"Shhh… I'm here… it's okay, Muñeca, I'm here," I coaxed the only thing that came to mind. Trusting it would work like it always did for her nightmares. Knowing this was just another one she was experiencing while she was awake.

"I love you," she wept, looking deep into my eyes. Searching for the man who would save her, not realizing he had been there this whole time.

That was another first for me, hearing her say those three words were as destructive as hearing her say she fucking hated me.

Her emotions got the best of me. I cleared my throat, whispering, "I know," before tucking her body against the nook of my arm and kissing her forehead one last time. I walked her toward the speedboat, about to watch her embark on her new life.

One that didn't include me.

I grabbed my sunglasses out of the front pocket of my jacket as we walked, not giving a fuck it was dark as shit out. Just needing the false security they provided. I pulled Amira in closer, squeezing her shoulder in reassurance. She was physically falling apart in my arms, and I was the one solely responsible for it. I couldn't do anything to take away her pain, and it was killing me more and more with each step that drew us closer to goodbye.

"No, man! I have no more room for her!" Álvaro hollered as soon as we were a few feet away.

Amira instantly lifted her head, darting her eyes to me. Unbelievably hopeful.

I didn't hesitate, not for one fucking second. "Alright, let me help you." I let go of her, pulling out my gun from the back of my jeans. Battling the craving to put a bullet between Alvaro's eyes for trying to play me for a fucking fool, but mostly for getting Amira's hopes up.

Instead, I glanced at the speedboat and aimed my gun toward the motherfucker's head sitting in one of the seats. I recognized him when we were walking up. He was as shady and corrupt as they come. Not batting an eye, I pulled the trigger, sending his body propelling back into the ocean. Immediately feeling better that he wouldn't be near Amira where he could do god knows what.

A few of the women screamed, holding on to each other for dear life. Except Amira. I think she was more shocked that I had just murdered a man for her freedom. Placing my gun back into its spot, I nodded to Alvaro who was suddenly pale as fuck.

"Looks like you just gained a spot," I arrogantly declared, unfazed by the pussy standing in front of me.

From the corner of my eye, I could see Amira was about to take off, but not because she was scared of me. She now understood how serious I was about getting her to safety. I hauled her over to me by her arm, kicking and screaming before she even had a chance to haul ass. Putting up one hell of a fight to escape. Whipping her body around, she desperately tried to get out of my hold.

"Jesus Christ, Amira! Enough!" I roared once I threw her over my shoulder.

"Let me go," she gritted, pulling at my arms. Scratching my hands, my back, anywhere she could. I barely wavered. "You don't want to do this! I know you don't want to send me away!"

"Amira, calm the fuck down!" I reasoned, only pissing her off further. Grabbing her by the wrists, halting her assault.

"Please! Please! I don't want to go! Don't do this, Damien! Please don't do this!" Her eyes were brimming with unshed tears, and my body twisted with nothing but longing to fall apart. To finally let out all the emotions that were wreaking havoc on my core.

Not just from tonight, but from every moment since we laid eyes on each other.

"I hate you! Do you hear me? I hate you!" she screamed, wanting to get some sort of reaction out of me.

I stepped onto the speedboat, wading through the sea of fifteen to twenty people to get to her seat. Taking a minute to wipe off the son of a bitch's blood with the sleeve of my jacket. As soon as I set her down, she crumbled in her seat. Looking out over at the water, not wanting to see me anymore. The slight breeze blew through her hair, visibly making her shiver. I ignored the stinging pain I felt from seeing her like that, it was minor compared to the pain she was feeling in her heart.

I crouched down in front of her, dodging her attempts to push me away, making her look at me instead. "I'm so fucking sorry…" I murmured, my voice breaking.

My heart shattering.

My world coming the fuck apart.

"One day, you'll understand that this was the best decision for you." With that, I kissed the top of her head for the last time, spun and left. Turning my back on the one girl who I loved with all my heart.

Our lives would forever change after that day.

Especially *mine*.

I didn't give a fuck what time it was, I went straight to a bar and drank until I felt numb. By the time I stumbled back to my apartment, it was into the wee hours of the morning. Fumbling with my keys to get the front door open. Failing miserably to hold myself together. Except, I wish I could tell you I was expecting what happened next…

But I didn't.

Not for one goddamn second.

15

Amira

I sat on the bed, taking in my surroundings. From the pictures on the walls, to the comforter below me, to the dark furniture that lined the room. My eyes couldn't focus on one thing for very long, it hurt too much. I don't know how long I sat there in that very spot, sinking deeper and deeper into the mattress, unable to move. Frozen in place.

I loved him.

I hated him.

Two conflicting feelings my heart couldn't take. I mostly loved him still, but I wanted to hate him even more.

I hugged my arms around my torso, shivering from the cold, or maybe it was from my heart being ripped away from me. The absence of his warmth that brought me so much security was long gone. I sat there in a state of shock, trying to wrap my head around why he would do this to me, to us. Why he thought this was the best decision for me. As if I was still a child and couldn't think for myself. I felt every emotion and then some, sitting in the dark room. It seemed so foreign, so unfamiliar or maybe that was just me. Feeling as though I had aged years and years in a short amount of time.

What would I do now?

I was beyond lost, not knowing which side was up, down, left, or right. Confused and disoriented among my own thoughts. Once again, the sanctuary in my mind was a void with nowhere to be found so I gave up, lying down on the bed that felt like a stranger's. Curling up into a ball, trying to seek comfort within my empty embrace. I shut my eyes. Unable to keep them open any longer. Extremely exhausted in every sense of the word. I must have passed out, letting the darkness creep over me. Suffocating any light that was left within me.

My eyes started to flutter open and they instantly darted to the shadowy figure I saw out of the corner of my eye, coming face to face with the man I thought I would never see again.

"Please, tell me I'm fucking hallucinating right now and you're not sleeping in my fucking bed," Damien rasped in a tone I didn't recognize.

The stench of alcohol immediately assaulted my senses. I could see his eyes were bloodshot red from the dim lighting of the moon. He was sitting in the armchair in the corner of his room, diagonally across from me. His lax body leaned back into the chair with his fingers perched against his lips.

I slowly sat up in the center of the bed, tucking my legs underneath me. Wrapping my arms around my torso, suddenly feeling cold again. Wishing the mattress would swallow me whole just to avoid the displeased expression on his face. Hating myself for disappointing him, yet again.

"If I told you I was an illusion, would you not be mad at me?" I questioned barely above a whisper.

He breathed out, shaking his head. "I'm way past mad. What the fuck, Amira? Do you have any idea how much planning it took to get you on that fucking boat?"

I muffled, "No, but I never asked you to do that."

"Excuse me? If you're going to show up at my fucking apartment, in my fucking bed you can't pussy out now. The damage is already fucking done. You're. Still. Here."

He didn't usually curse at me like this, or at least not this much. I assumed it had to be the liquor talking or he was just exceedingly upset with me. I chose to believe the first one.

"I said no. But I didn't ask you to do that," I repeated, louder that time.

He chuckled, rubbing his fingers along the ridges of his lips. "Un-fucking-believable. What did you do? Jump off the boat?"

"No. I just waited for you to leave and before the boat pushed back from the dock, I nicely asked the gentleman if he would let me off."

"Nicely, eh?"

"Yeah. He just watched you kill someone at point blank. It was a good introduction for me, and it worked in my favor. God rest his soul. The man was scared of you, so he let me go."

"If he had been scared of me, he wouldn't have dared to let you off that fucking boat. Besides, that motherfucker had it coming. He was corrupt as fuck. He's lucky to have survived that long. Don't worry, his soul was already resting in Hell before my fucking bullet hit his head."

I swallowed hard, nodding.

"I don't murder innocent people, Muñeca."

"But you do murder people?" I blurted, regretting the question as soon as it left my mouth. "You don't have to answer that."

"Why? Because you suddenly don't want to know my truths and fucking business?"

I shook my head. "I just know you don't like answering my questions."

"I see, so you've become obedient in the last few hours. Might have meant something if you actually stayed on the goddamn boat."

I didn't say anything because what could I say to that?

"How did you get in?"

My eyes widened, not wanting to tell him.

"Don't make me ask you again, Amira."

I didn't. He was being the calm Damien again, although he was burning inside.

From me.

I loved it…

And I hated it.

But I loved it more, I think.

"With a key, I stole it from Mama Rosa's keychain when I noticed she had a spare."

"So now you're a liar and a thief?" he insolently stated, even though it came out as a question.

I winced, hugging myself tighter. "I was just trying to have a backup plan. In case I ever needed to run from Mama Rosa's house and hide."

His face went sullen as he narrowed his eyes at me. "Why didn't you tell me that?"

"Sometimes I don't tell you things."

"Since when? Most of the time I can't get you to shut the fuck up." He placed his index finger out in front of his lips. "I'm sorry, Muñeca. I didn't mean that. It's been a long fucking day, and I'm hanging on by a thread here. Do you understand me?"

"Yes. You say shitty things when you're mad or upset. Almost like a child throwing a temper tantrum," I replied, showing him I could say mean things too.

He grinned. "Did you ever stop and think those are the kinds of things I needed to know?"

"Yes. Which is why I didn't tell you. I didn't want you to worry about me. You already do enough of that. I mean, look what you did tonight. You were trying to send me away—"

He was over to me in three strides, standing near the edge of the bed, slamming his fists into the mattress between us. “For the last fucking time, I was not sending you away!”

I didn’t falter. If I did, I would lose. I made my way over to him on my hands and knees, stopping when our faces were inches apart.

Adamantly countering, “That’s what it felt like to me. All you do is make choices for me. What I need, what I want, how I feel… it’s bullshit! I’m not a little girl anymore, if I ever truly was one. I’ve lived through my own darkness and watched you battle yours for years. I may not know exactly what you do, but know I don’t have to wonder. You showed me tonight. And you want to know something? I don’t care! It’s not who you are. It’s who you think you have to be!”

He jerked back like I had slapped him across the face. I knew it was the liquor lowering his guard. He would’ve never showed me his emotions otherwise. That wasn’t who Damien was, and I’d be damned if I wasn’t going to use it to my advantage. Standing up for what I believed in and felt in my heart.

“Don’t ever do that to me again! Do you understand me?” I repeated the statement he always said to me with the same hard edge in my tone. “We’re in this life together for the long run. Whether it’s in Cuba under Emilio Salazar’s “Fatherland”, or in any other part of the world under Damien Montero’s demons. We’re family. *You’re*”—I stabbed my finger over his heart, moving to stand in front of him— “my family. And we don’t turn our backs on each other. Ever!” I paused, allowing what I said to sink into his thick, stubborn skull. “I love you, and I know you love me. I’ve known you loved me every second of every single day for almost six years. I don’t need to hear you say it. They’re just words. Your actions have always spoken louder than any of those endearments. The older I’ve gotten, the more I’ve realized that I’m in love with you. I’ve been in love with you as long as I can remember.”

“Amira—”

In that moment.

In that minute.

I kissed him.

Even though I had no experience, no knowledge, no anything of what I was doing. I couldn't help myself. I had to feel his lips on mine. I had to show him, prove to him that he loved me as much as I loved him. He was just too scared to think it, to feel it, to act on it, so I did it for him. Wanting him to finally see me as the young woman I was, and not the little girl he saved.

I didn't need saving anymore.

He did.

The second I parted my lips, he roughly gripped onto my hair by the nook of my neck. Crudely yanking my head back and off his mouth. I gasped, feeling the intrusion on my scalp in a heavenly and sinful sensation. My chest was rising and falling as I stared into his eyes, dark and dilated in a mesmerizing way. Captivating every last part of me from my head down to the tips of my toes, and all he was doing was glaring at me. Clinging to my core in the exact manner he was clutching onto my hair. I didn't move an inch. Panicked that if I did, he would stop and I would never get to experience him looking at me like that again.

"Please," I panted for I don't know what.

Baiting him. Tempting him. Breaking him.

And then I saw it.

Clear as day.

The thin string he talked about minutes ago, snapped.

It was loud.

It was chaotic.

It was everything I ever wanted.

Him.

He growled from deep within his chest, crashing his mouth onto mine. Clutching the side of my face with his hands, he bit my bottom lip. Unmercifully slamming me hard into the wall behind us, causing my mouth to fly open from the pleasure and pain of his touch. He growled again, but this time he plunged his dominant, hot tongue into my awaiting and willing mouth. Teasing me with the tip, all along the outline of my lips. Seeking out my tongue.

My senses heightened, taking in the scent of cigarettes, and that sweet, malty taste of the alcohol that lingered in his mouth. I would never be able to smell that scent without thinking about Damien in this very moment.

The taste of him.

The feel of him.

The scent of him.

Was all around me…

Branding itself into every pore of my body. Hundreds of thoughts and questions crossed my mind, but it didn't matter because my heart already knew the answers.

There was something agonizing and desperate in the way his mouth moved against mine, as I tried to follow the momentum of his lips. My hands reached up, trying to touch him, but he intercepted them. Gripping both of my wrists in one of his hands, placing them above my head on the wall.

He couldn't let me touch him.

He wouldn't be able to control himself.

And Damien was all about control, even though he was losing himself with me, right then and there.

His grasp burned against my wrists. Searing and scarring me in ways I may never be able to recover from. With his other fingers, he ran them down the length of my arm, stopping when he reached my face. It felt like he wanted to caress my body, cup my breasts, and make me moan from his touch.

Make. Me. His.

Instead, he brushed my cheek and down the back of my neck. Pulling me closer to him, but not nearly close enough. I wanted him to mold us into one person, forever a part of one another. My body curved into his as my inexperienced tongue pushed into his mouth, causing him to groan at the taste of me. I tried to follow each and every lead he was giving me. Praying I was doing it justice, having the same effect on him that he was on me.

"Damien…" I moaned, causing him to simultaneously pull away.

He released my wrists, and I whimpered at the loss of his warmth as he placed his hands on the sides of my face. Caging me in with his arms, everything felt right and I never wanted to leave. He hovered above me, panting for air. Both of us trying to find our bearings. I didn't want to open my eyes, terrified that this would be an illusion of my lovestruck mind. It wasn't until I finally opened them that I saw what I had so urgently needed to see.

Love.

His love for *me.*

Just as quickly as I saw it, he turned and left. Fully aware that he let his guard down, allowing me in. For the first time in his life, *I* controlled him. Even if it was only for a few minutes.

Petrifying him more than anything had in a long time.

He was mine.

And I had always known that…

16

Amira

After our kiss, he left. I didn't feel the need to follow after him, mostly because I knew a part of me still lingered on his mouth. I just laid back down on his bed, making myself comfortable, incessantly rubbing my fingers over my swollen lips. Tasting him all over again, and he wasn't even there. I thought about Damien in a way I never had before, and it put a smile on my face. A different kind of smile. In that moment, I felt older. More mature in my fifteen-year-old skin. It was amazing how one kiss could instantly change a girl, and I was no exception.

The sound of Damien's footsteps coming down the hall, back into his room, brought me out of my desirable, pleasurable thoughts. I instantly rolled over to my side, putting my back toward the door. Pretending like I was sleeping. I heard him shuffling around, opening and closing drawers. Making his way into the en-suite bathroom and turning on the shower. There was something mischievous about knowing Damien was only a few feet away naked, vulnerable, and exposed. The feeling sent tingles to all sorts of uncharted places on my body, mind, and soul. It thrilled me, filling my mind with thoughts I never considered before that night.

The bathroom door opened minutes later, and out walked Damien filling the space with steam and his masculine fresh scent. He shut all the blinds and curtains, making sure the early morning dawn disappeared, and possibly the world too. Replacing it with the comfort of the darkness that we were both acquainted to. The way he effortlessly moved around the room, made me wonder if he'd spent a lot of mornings just like this. Coming home when the sun was starting its day. A sense of jealously washed over me, thinking he was with a woman, and if she had been lying where I was right now.

Waiting for him like me.

As soon as I felt the bed dip behind me, I stopped thinking. At least about his other conquests. Once again waiting for his next move. Nothing happened for what felt like forever, but I swear I could feel his conflicting emotions soaring through me. As if I was the one experiencing them firsthand. I inadvertently began to follow the soft rhythm of his breathing like I did every time after a nightmare had reared its ugly head. The gentle lull slowly rocked me back to sleep. Before I knew it, I was dozing off, about to slip into a deep sleep when I thought I felt his arm wrap around my stomach, turning me over to rest my head on his chest.

I sighed in contentment, melting into his warm frame. Allowing myself to relax under his feather touch as he lazily rubbed my back and played with my hair like all he needed was to have me close to his heart.

I was convinced I must have been dreaming because I woke up the next afternoon alone. My eyes sleepily searched the room for any sign of Damien. He wasn't there.

The smell of coffee flowed into the bedroom, lifting me from my blissful haze. I sat up, taking a second to stretch, still exhausted from the night's events. Wanting to hop in the shower to rinse away the filth I felt coating my skin, I figured it might be better to give Damien more alone time that he obviously desired. I jumped into the warm water cascading from the showerhead above, not taking long to wash my hair and body. Using all of Damien's toiletries made me giddy. Knowing I would be able to take home his scent on every inch of my skin.

I grabbed a towel when I was done, wrapping it around my chest, and made my way toward his bedroom. Deciding at the last second to grab one of his crème button-down shirts from his closet, instead.

My wet hair was dripping down his shirt making me shiver, but I didn't care. I wanted to go to him.

He was outside leaning against the balcony railing with his back to me, lost in thought. I hated seeing him like that. It was the worst feeling in the world. He didn't hear me approach as I snuck up behind him, wrapping my arms around his muscular torso. Causing him to stiffen from my embrace. He instantly grabbed a hold of my wrists, dropping my arms to the side, and walked back into his apartment without saying a word. Rejecting my touch.

He had never done that before.

I stepped back inside. "Hey…"

He froze in his living room, taking a second to turn around to face me. His eyes immediately roamed my body. I never wanted to know what he was thinking more than in that second, but he hadn't met my eyes yet.

Until he did.

He looked exhausted, as if he hadn't slept at all, but that wasn't what had my attention. It was the fact that his kind, honey-colored eyes looked dark with no light in them whatsoever.

He suddenly cocked his head to the side, rasping, "Did I say you could wear my shirt? Looking like one of my whores doesn't suit you, Muñeca."

I jerked back from the forceful impact of his words. My smile fell from my lips as he stared at me harshly.

"You shouldn't wear a man's shirt when you don't belong to him," he added, never taking his eyes off mine.

"Damien… please don't do this," I whispered, loathing I had to say that after everything that happened last night. I thought today would be different.

We would be different.

"You know, for a smart fucking girl you haven't been paying attention. This is who I am. I get drunk and fuck whores, not little girls."

I shook my head in disbelief. "So, this is how it's going to be now? Why? Because you love me? So what? You have to push me away? Oh, come on, Damien, I'm a hell of a lot smarter than that."

"Don't confuse lust for love, Amira. I was drunk, you were here. It was one kiss that did nothing for my cock. Now you all of a sudden think I'm in love with you? Don't be so fucking naive, little girl. You should be thanking me for giving you your first introduction to men. Not giving me shit for it."

I scoffed, stunned that he was doing this to me again. Trying to reign in my pain, I declared in a steady voice, "You know what? I don't have to stand here and take this. You do whatever you need to do to cool off. When you're ready to really talk about what's happening between us, you know where I am." I shoved past him, wanting to get out of there and away from him as fast as possible. Knowing this would blow over as soon as he realized how he'd treated me. He just needed more time to reflect on our future.

Right when I had almost fully passed him, he grabbed my arm. Turning me to look at him. He calmly vowed, "We can't talk about what's not real."

I yanked my arm out of his grasp and stormed down the hallway. One way or another after last night with him forcing me on the boat, me showing up at his apartment, then the kiss, and everything else in between. It would change our relationship, proving it that morning. I didn't realize until days, weeks, months later that all I did that morning by leaving him was exactly what he wanted me to do in the first place.

I played right into the hand of cards he dealt me.

In exactly one year's time, since the night of our kiss, everything had shifted. Taking on a course of its own. Nothing would ever be the same again, and I wished I would've known that the next morning. I could've been more prepared for what was to come.

But I wasn't.

I never was with him.

Damien started to work more, and I saw him less and less as the months flew by. There were times I wouldn't see him for weeks on end, showing up sporadically, and never as the man I was in love with. He barely said more than a few words to me, if that. He didn't take the time to talk to me about life, never asked me about my day, and he quit practicing all the languages and assignments I struggled with.

Nothing.

At first, I continued placing random things in his belongings, and every time he returned Yuly it gave me hope that maybe he would make his way back to me. Then out of nowhere, he didn't return her. Breaking any connection with us. Most of the time, I wondered why he even bothered to stop by Mama Rosa's. Other than to eat some food and leave shortly after. He completely shut me out of his life. I couldn't even look in his eyes anymore. All that stared back at me were vacant, dark pools of the man who once saved me. He stopped communicating where he was going and when he'd return. Leaving me to sit in my reading nook worried, contemplating if he was dead or alive. Staring aimlessly out the window, hoping at any second one of the passing cars would be his.

But he never came.

I no longer made him laugh or smile. I'd tried to tease him, hoping he would let me in. Put his hands on me and make me feel like I was whole again. However, he barely glanced my way, as if I was nothing but a burden to him. Reminding me of the time he admitted that I was. I had no idea who this man was anymore, and maybe I never had.

Which was the hardest confession I admitted to myself.

My nightmares started to resurface again, except they were different. It wasn't Emilio's or his men, or even his father's faces that tormented me. Mixing along with my family's desperate pleas to save them.

It was Damien's.

Just like in the land of the living, he would stand there. Not paying me any mind, letting them torture me, grab me, and take me to the depths of Hell with them. The images became so real, so vivid, so alive… To the point that Mamá Rosa couldn't wake me, no matter how hard she tried. My night terrors had taken over, and I barely slept more than a few hours every night. It was easier to stare up at the ceiling than it was to close my eyes, surrendering to the darkness that had become my daily life. Versus the one's in my nightmares.

I no longer had any peace.

Damien had stolen it.

I missed him. I missed him so much it hurt to think about all those years where he was my one and only. As the months went on, more questions, more what if's, more regrets and mistakes made themselves known. Surfacing deep within my heart.

Should I have stayed on the boat?

Would we have met again later in life and been happy?

Should I have not kissed him?

My thoughts ruthlessly weighed on my mind, sending me spiraling down a staircase to Hell. Where the devil welcomed me with open arms. The same purgatory Damien spent years trying to protect me from was the same one he exiled me to solely by himself.

The irony was not lost on me.

See, Damien knew I could battle his anger, the brutality of his words, aware that I wasn't intimidated or scared of him. But I couldn't fight for what wasn't there.

His silence.

His coldness.

His distant hollowness.

Were all weapons I had no artillery for.

Like the little girl he probably still thought I was, I held onto the hope that today would be different. That he wouldn't do this to me.

Not after everything he had done to destroy my heart, or the stuff he was still putting me through. He always made sure to be there for my birthday, giving me the best gifts, the most attention. Showing me that I mattered to someone.

To him.

It was my sixteenth birthday, and I waited all day for him. Praying that he would show up for me, knowing how important it was to have him there by my side. I didn't think he'd be this cruel. It didn't help my situation that one year ago today triggered the drastic change in him. I couldn't just mope around and continue to feel this way. I needed answers, and I needed them right now.

I took a cab down to his University. It was the only place that seemed to occupy all his time from before. It was a long shot, but what other choice did I have? I took my chance that he'd be there.

I sat in the backseat wringing my fingers together, rehearsing what I wanted to say to him in my head. Picturing better times when he'd come over and we'd talk about his classes for hours, filling me in on all the interesting material he had learned. Always so adamant that I would go to college too.

I asked the driver if he could just drive around the law school grounds, keeping my fingers crossed that I would find him. I guess luck was on my side that evening because after only fifteen minutes of searching, there he was, stepping out of his car. I ordered the driver to stop, throwing cash in his lap and rushing out the door before the vehicle had come to a complete stop. Drawing attention to myself because Damien instantly glanced in my direction as I shut the door behind me.

I hadn't seen him in weeks. He looked older, tired, but still handsome as ever. His hair was tied up in a bun high on his head. His facial hair grew longer, only adding to his dangerous allure. Though it was his innocent face that let him get away with whatever the hell he was involved in for Emilio. I assumed no one ever saw him coming, until it was too late. His muscular frame appeared bigger, stockier, more dominant; it loomed over my small build as I made my way over to him.

“Hey,” I greeted, not knowing what else to say.

My mind suddenly drew a blank from his authoritative and commanding presence hovering above me. He was so tall compared to my five-feet-four figure, feeling every bit of his six-feet-four stature. I wanted to hug him, embrace him, something other than this abrupt welcome like two strangers meeting for the first time. He didn’t move, obviously not reciprocating my same sentiment, even though it was my birthday.

A day he always celebrated with me.

“What are you doing here, Amira?” he callously questioned which shouldn’t have surprised me, but it did.

“Do you know what today is?”

“Yes.”

My heart sped up, and I warily smiled at him.

“It’s Wednesday, and I have a criminal law class in five minutes, and your unannounced little visit is going to make me run late for it.”

I winced, but he didn’t even bat an eye. “It’s my birthday, Damien,” I informed, hoping for an iota of warmth.

“To me it’s just another day for you to want something. So what the fuck can I do for you now?”

“You could stop being a fucking asshole!” I snapped, probably giving him exactly what he wanted, but I didn’t care anymore. If he wanted me to speak my mind and tell him what I wanted, then I was going to do precisely that. “One year! Three hundred and sixty-five days and I don’t know how many hours because I can’t do math that quickly. But you already know that! And it would’ve made you laugh, if you hadn’t permanently wedged a stick so far up your ass I’m surprised you can even walk still! All you do is throw low fucking blows at me!”

In one stride, he was in my face. “Don’t you ever cuss or raise your tone to me again,” he steadily ordered. “Do you understand me?”

I blinked, smiling. Knowing exactly what I was about to say. Standing on the tips of my toes to try to get as close to his face as I could, I spewed, "Fuck. You!"

He leaned in closer, an inch away from my lips. My mind started racing, mimicking my rapidly beating heart. I thought he was going to kiss me, so when he murmured, "You're damn lucky we're on school grounds because if we were anywhere else in public, I wouldn't think twice about taking you over my knee and teaching you a thing or two about some fucking manners."

I didn't know what was worse, that he didn't kiss me or that I wanted him to do exactly what he just threatened.

"Now, turn your ass around and go fucking home, Amira. Nothing good happens to little girls who are out this late at night."

He meant it as a dig, but the truth was he just revealed a crack in his façade. Damien wanted me to go because he was still protective over me, and as soon as he recognized what he did, he blinked, shoving it all away. I swallowed hard, resisting the urge to kiss him again. Not caring what might happen after this time. It couldn't get any worse.

Oh, how wrong I was…

"You asked me what you could do for me today, right?"

He narrowed his eyes at me, taking in my words.

"I want you to call me Muñeca. You haven't called me that in so long." I licked my lips, baiting him. His stare followed the movement of my tongue. "Then I want you to kiss me and prove to me that you don't still feel this connection that's always been between us."

He subtly grinned. "Look at you, Amira. Making demands. It's really fucking cute, actually. I'd gladly oblige just to prove you wrong, but I don't think my girlfriend would appreciate that."

My head flew back, stepping away from him. "Your girlfriend? Since when do you have a girlfriend?"

"Since I wanted to get my dick sucked on a regular basis. We're done here." He gave me a curt nod. "Go home." With that, he turned and left.

Leaving me there speechless, feeling as though the ground was crawling up my legs and eating me whole. I went home, empty and alone. Avoiding Mama Rosa at all costs. She knew. I never told her what had happened with Damien. It was clear as day. I think part of her hated him for it as much as I did.

I laid in my bed, staring at my ceiling for I don't know how long. Repeating the last thing he said to me in my head. Contemplating if he was just lying to me so I would go and stay away from him. I peered around my room, taking in every gift he'd ever gotten me throughout the years. My eyes stopped when they reached an open space on the shelf of dolls. For some reason it made me angry, not seeing Yuly among them. Missing the one thing he didn't provide for me.

I got out of bed, slipping on a hoodie and my shoes. Quietly opening my door so I wouldn't wake Mama Rosa. Deciding that I wanted to get Yuly now, he didn't deserve her anymore. I made it out of the house with no problem, hailing another cab over to his apartment. I was grateful I still had his key, hoping he hadn't changed the locks on me. Especially since he knew why I had taken it from Mama Rosa in the first place. At this point, nothing would surprise me, though.

We pulled up just outside his door around eleven o'clock at night. Only reminding me of the last time I was here this late. I stepped out hearing a blend of loud music surrounding the complex, thinking someone was having one hell of a party. As soon as I unlocked his door, the music became a little louder. Suddenly realizing its origin was coming from his room. My feet moved on their own accord, having no control over the movement of my limbs. Each calculated step pulled me closer to his bedroom, to his bed, to the girlfriend he was touching, kissing, and making love to.

When it was always supposed to be me.

My stomach was in knots, my heart was in my throat, and I swear I felt like I was going to either throw up or pass out. My anxiety for what was to come lived and breathed in my blood. It pumped in my veins and produced a piercing vibration at my temples. I ignored the looming feeling that I felt in the depths of my soul. Pressing my fingers to my lips, feeling the last place he ever touched me. It fabricated a false illusion that he was still mine, even though something told me he never was to begin with.

The closer I got, the louder her moans became. Mixed somewhere between pleasure and pain. I barely had time to contemplate what I was doing, before I was standing in the doorway witnessing yet another one of my worst nightmares. I swear I stopped breathing, and a rush of adrenaline shot through my core. It was like witnessing a tragic accident, wanting so badly to look away, but I couldn't take my stare off the vision before me. She was on all fours, naked at the edge of the bed. Left in nothing but black stiletto high heels. Her wrists were handcuffed out in front of her, and there was a blindfold over her eyes. Damien was behind her, fisting her hair and yanking her head back as he roughly thrust in and out of her. Each movement driving another dagger deep into my heart.

I couldn't help how my eyes gravitated toward his muscular, toned physique. I took in every curve, regarded every cut ab, how he had these V lines in his lower abdomen. The way the sweat glistened off his body in the moonlight, pooling at his temples. How his long, wavy brown hair was slicked back, accentuating his chiseled jaw that tensed with every movement of his tight body. Down to the way his fingers dug into her voluptuous hips.

I shut my eyes, glancing back at her instead. Feeling my eyes begin to water from the scene unfolding in front of me, I immediately blinked and shook them away as rapidly as they appeared. Hearing the smacking sound of their skin on skin contact, bringing me right back to the reality that was in front of me. I watched with unforgiving eyes as he manipulated and controlled her body.

Her pleasure.

All of it.

Even her mind.

It was animalistic and primal the way he was vigorously taking her from behind.

The pain I experienced was like being on the receiving end of a loaded gun. I just never imagined that Damien would be the one aiming it at me. It wasn't until I heard her yell out, "I love you!" her body shaking profusely, that I loudly gasped.

Damien immediately looked up, and I placed my hand over my mouth, realizing what I had just done. His eyes locked with mine, staying like that for several seconds. Or it could've been hours, time just sort of stood still as tears streamed down my face. There was no controlling them any longer.

He didn't even bother pulling out of her as his dark, vacant pools continued barring into mine. Not providing me any of the comfort he knew I needed more than ever before. His girlfriend didn't even hear me, lost in her own euphoria. I didn't bother wiping away my tears, I wanted him to see my heart breaking, feel it bleeding out in front of him. And for a split-second, I thought he did. Right when I felt his eyes starting to turn into the man's I needed, he blinked it away.

Firmly gripping onto his girlfriend's hips with so much force, passionately thrusting into her again. He snaked his hand that was fisting her hair to the front of her neck, pulling her back against his chest by her throat. Not letting go of his hold, he used his other hand to control the rhythm of her hips. Making her sway her ass on him like they were doing an intimate, sinful dance. He was no longer just fucking her; he was now making love to her.

Seeing their bodies joined together like that, in such a familiar way, was one of the hardest things I'd ever have to see. He waited until I saw what he was doing, until he had a direct shot at my heart, until he knew I felt like I couldn't breathe.

Until…

Until…

Until…

He started to run his nose along the side of her neck, gently trailing kisses, never breaking our connection. Controlling me in the same way he was her. It was as if he was fucking with my heart and mind while he was fucking her from behind. I should've expected what happened next, but I didn't.

Finally proving to me that he really was another monster after all.

As soon as he reached her ear, he sucked it between his teeth and growled, "I love you, too, mi luz." He called her *his* light.

Pulling the trigger into my heart.

Finishing me off completely.

17

Damien

I walked into Rosarío's house with my girl, Evita, clinging to my arm. Nervously fidgeting with a strand of her blonde hair. It was the first time I was introducing a woman to my family. Between her and Rosarío constantly riding my ass, wanting to meet one another for the last year and a half, I had no choice but to finally cave. Even though it was the last thing I wanted to fucking do. Don't get me wrong, I loved Evita—she was sweet, funny, humble. Not to mention, she was fucking gorgeous. She was five-feet-six and had legs that went on for days.

The problem laid with not wanting to hurt Amira anymore. I had already done enough of that for a lifetime. Since the night she walked in on me fucking Evita over a year ago, Amira officially backed the fuck off. She stopped calling, dropping by, and asking Rosarío about me. Anytime I'd come to visit, she either wasn't around, or wouldn't come out of her room. When she did, it was like I wasn't even there. I was no longer the center of her world, and I had no one to blame but myself.

There was only one thing that became fucking clear after she got off the boat, over two years ago. The only way I could protect her was to stay the fuck away from her. She was safer without me constantly in her life, fantasizing about me in situations that would never happen in reality. There was no way in hell we could ever be together. My life revolved around Emilio Salazar, and I tried for too fucking long to make them both coexist in my life. I was so goddamn selfish. I greedily took the light that only she could provide me, but didn't stop for one minute to see what I was actually doing to her. Exposing her to more danger than keeping her safe.

My protection for Amira now was to push her away, even though it almost fucking killed me to do so. I didn't expect her to show up at my school that night. It only proved that she was still fighting a battle she never had a chance of winning. After her blatant display of not backing down, no matter how cold or shitty I treated her, I knew I had no choice but to put an end to it all.

Her memories of me.

Her illusions of what we could never be.

Especially the love and devotion she still felt for me.

I was completely aware that Amira would show up at my apartment later that night. I knew her like the back of my fucking hand. I would never forget the look on her face when she saw me purposely fuck Evita in front of her. I hated having to use another woman to destroy Amira, but she left me no other choice.

I never claimed to be anything I wasn't. I always told Amira—I was just another fucking monster taking up space in her life. Finally, proving it to her that very night.

Besides, from day one, I gave her Rosarío. Her guardianship was all she ever needed.

She was her family.

Not me.

As much as I wanted to chase after Amira when she ran out of my room and out of my life forever, I couldn't. I was done being the man she needed me to be.

In the end, it all worked out. Emilio stopped sniffing his nose where it didn't fucking belong. My father didn't dare to mention anything to anyone about Amira, including me. And meeting Evita, allowing myself to care and love another woman, who wasn't Amira, for the first time in my life.

I met Evita at school, purely on accident. We bumped into each other at the library one night when we were both studying late. She was reaching for a book on the top shelf, and I wasn't paying attention to where I was going. Colliding into the most beautiful girl on campus. She was naturally flawless and innocent, much like Amira. I was instantly drawn to her, probably because she reminded me of the little girl I had once saved. Her family had died in a tragic car accident when she was a teenager. Leaving her an orphan and completely alone. We bonded over a similar darkness, the way Amira and I had.

Evita knew from day one what I did every day when I wasn't in school. There was no point in lying to her about it. She never judged my decisions or questioned my actions. Instead, she fell in love with me almost immediately. I wish I could say the feeling was mutual at first, however it wasn't. I cared for her deeply and would do anything for her. It was hard not to. We'd been officially a couple since the first time I fucked her, after a whole month of dating upon her request. The longest thirty days of my fucking existence. I was the second man she'd ever been with, and she wanted to wait. On day thirty-one, she finally agreed to let me fuck her twelve ways to Sunday. I swear we didn't leave my bed for a week.

By the time Amira showed up at my school, we'd been together over six months. The first time I told Evita I loved her was when Amira was staring into my dark, soulless goddamn eyes.

I was a fucking monster.

Evita couldn't have been happier hearing those three words that night. When all I could think about was Amira's face as she rushed out, leaving behind her broken heart that I would eternally hold in the palm of my hand.

I'd spent the rest of night out on the balcony with Yuly in my hands, while Evita slept in my bed. Needing to feel close to Amira the only way I knew how. The water would always be our connection to one another. She loved it as much as I did. Along with the night sky after she told me the Andromeda and Perseus love story all those years ago. On nights like these I'd catch myself searching for their constellation, thinking Amira was staring at the same sky at that exact moment. Thinking back to before everything went awry.

I knew the very next morning after she kissed me, I was going to have to show her the man I'd always been. We could never happen, I had to push her away by betraying and hurting her to the point that she would walk away from me because God knows, I wasn't strong enough to stay away from her.

Except, I allowed myself to walk back into my bedroom to fucking hold her one last time. She wasn't sleeping when I sat on the bed next to her, so I waited until her breathing evened and I knew she'd passed out. Not wanting to fuck with her head any more than I already had, knowing what I was about to do would destroy her. I pulled her toward me, placing the side of her body right on my chest, desperately resisting the urge to kiss her again. Touch her, fucking devour her. I was content in just holding her against me. Rubbing her back like I had done so many damn times before. Still feeling her everywhere, especially in my dark fucking heart.

Of course, I fucking loved her. I always knew it, but it was easier to deny such feelings until I couldn't do it anymore. She almost knocked me on my ass when she kissed me, never thinking she would have the balls to do that. Which was one of the many reasons I loved her. She wasn't scared of me, she'd never been fucking scared of me. Soon that would change, and she would hate me. Nothing would ever go back to the way it was between us after that night. I never hated myself more for what I did to her. I swear on everything fucking holy, all I wanted to do was to make it right by Amira.

Knowing I would never be able to do just that.

One thing inside of me did change after that night, I allowed myself to actually fall in love with Evita. Closing one chapter of my life to open another. She deserved it, earning my trust. I thought maybe I could start making love to her and finally let my guard down in that way.

I couldn't.

Not that I didn't try. It was just something that would forever be a part of me, no matter how much I wanted to set it aside. Evita loved it when I fucked her, dominated her, controlled every last part of her body, mind, and soul. So it wasn't an issue.

At least not for her.

"Damien! There you are! Late as always," Rosarío greeted when she saw us walk into the living room, pulling me into a tight hug.

I kissed her cheek, backing away. Evita's grasp tightened around my arm. Tugging my hair away from my face, I announced, "Rosarío, this is—"

"I know who this is," she interrupted, grabbing Evita's shoulders to take a good look at her. Thank God, I warned her that Rosarío was like my mother and she was as affectionate as they came. "I have heard so much about you, Evita. You're just as gorgeous as I knew you would be."

"Thank you so much. I've heard so much about you too. It's so wonderful to finally meet you," Evita replied, kissing Rosarío's cheek.

"We have much to catch up on. I've been telling Damien for months to bring you over, but you know him… stubborn as a mule."

Evita smiled, glancing over at me. "So I'm not the only one who thinks that?"

I glared at her, making them both laugh. Trying to mask the desire to look around for Amira, silently hoping she wouldn't be here, but at the same time, wishing she was. I couldn't even remember the last time I saw her. I stopped by for her seventeenth birthday, but she was nowhere to be found. As if she knew I was coming.

Eternally feeling me too.

"I know Damien said not to make a big deal about you coming over, Evita, but I'm sorry… I couldn't resist. I invited some friends, I may have a pig in the oven, and there's possibly some torticas de moron baking in there as well. I mean, I'm just saying."

"Rosarío—"

"Oh, it's fine, Damien," Evita cut me off, placing her hand on my chest. "I would love to meet more of your friends and family."

Rosarío beamed. "I like her already, Damien."

"At least one of us does right now," I scoffed, earning myself a smack on the back of my head by Rosarío.

Her friends arrived shortly after and spent the rest of the afternoon in the kitchen, drinking entirely way too much, eating and talking all about me. Evita asked too many fucking questions about my childhood, from how I was raised, to what I loved doing the most, to God knows what else. Rosarío and her friends were all too delighted to oblige. I was waiting for Rosarío to pull out the album of baby pictures, but I think she knew better. I tuned them out after a while, aimlessly staring out at Amira's garden as I leaned against the sliding glass door. All her Mariposa flowers were dead, withered away like no one had taken care of them for months.

"Babe… what are you doing all the way over here?" Evita slightly slurred, throwing her arms around my neck. "You look all Damien-like. Lost in thought."

"You're drunk," I simply stated, grabbing ahold of her waist to help hold her up.

"I thought you liked it when I got drunk, so you can do naughty things to me."

"I don't need you drunk to do things to you, Evita."

She smiled, loudly replying, "I want you to do things to me now!"

"Shhh, enough of that."

"Oh, come on, babe. I love Rosarío! I love all her friends, and I love you so much!"

"Evita, I mean it. Enough."

"Hey!" She stepped back, out of my arms. "Rosarío would be more than excited if we had babies!" She glanced back at her. "Wouldn't you, Rosarío?"

Rosarío took one look at me and then back at her, narrowing her eyes at us. Waiting for the other fucking shoe to drop. As soon as I stepped toward Evita to shut her mouth for her, she drunkenly blurted what we weren't going to announce yet.

"I'm your fiancée now! Everyone will want us to make babies!"

Before she even got the last word out, my eyes inadvertently shifted to Amira's garden. Locking eyes with my Muñeca. It was like she appeared out of thin air at the worse time possible. My heart fucking stopped from the expression on her face, rendering me fucking speechless. Knowing she'd just heard everything from the open slider door.

"Oh! We weren't supposed to tell you yet! Shit!" Evita exclaimed, stepping into my arms again. Looking up at me through her long lashes, she said, "I'm sorry, babe. The wine, the excitement, and everyone got the best of me. How could I ever make this up to you?" She nervously laughed, trying to bring my attention back to her. Though it was solely focused on the girl frozen in place, a few steps in front of me.

"You're engaged?" Rosarío called out, and even her voice couldn't tear me away from Amira's intense gaze.

"Yeah!" Evita replied, turning to face them. "He asked me to marry him a few weeks ago. I said yes! It was probably the only reason he finally let us meet."

"Oh my God!" Rosarío excitedly screamed, and everyone followed suit.

What happened next was one big blur. Everyone faded into the distance as they celebrated our engagement. No one noticed the tsunami of emotions drowning both Amira and me. My whole world seemed to come crashing down on me in a matter of seconds.

Everything I thought I knew, everything I wanted to believe in, all of it…

Gone.

18

Damien

We stayed there lost in time, locked in each other's gaze for what felt like a lifetime. I needed to snap out of it, but I couldn't tear my eyes away from her. She had matured so much since the last time I saw her. She was almost unrecognizable. No longer a girl but a woman. My boots were cemented to the spot I was standing in while chaos erupted all around us.

And I wasn't talking about the celebration.

My control…

Was long fucking gone.

"Amira!" Rosarío shouted, making everyone turn to look at her.

She was the first to break our trance-like state of mind, shaking her head as Rosarío rushed over to her. "Hi, Mama Rosa."

"Mamita, are you okay—"

"Of course," she breathed out, falsely smiling. "I just thought I'd stop in to say hello to everyone on my way to the movies. From the noise, I guess it's a good thing I did." She gazed back over at us, and it was only then I realized Evita was in my arms, looking over at Amira. Making the situation even more awkward.

"I hear congratulations is in order!" she coaxed, walking over to us.

I could see the distress written over her face and the change in her demeanor, as much as she tried to hide it. There was no way she could hide from me. She was still hopelessly in love with me, and I would be lying if I said I didn't already know she never stopped.

"You're Amira?" Evita asked, when she was standing in front of us.

"I am."

"So nice to finally meet you! Damien told me you're Rosarío's niece."

"Mmm hmm."

"You're beautiful! Oh my God, Damien, why didn't you tell me she's a knock out! I bet you make the boys crazy!"

"Not boys. Just a boy," Amira retorted, almost knocking me on my ass.

"What boy? Rosarío never told me you were dating anyone," I questioned, trying to conceal the hard edge in my voice.

"Oh, Damien," Rosarío chimed in, moving to stand beside us. "He's always been so protective over her. He still can't see that our Amira isn't a little girl anymore. I mean look at her, do you see? She's a woman now."

"Oh, I see," I gritted out, seeing fucking red.

Amira cunningly grinned, aware of the sudden tension in my tone. "Actually, I don't think he's considered a boy anymore, Evita. He's twenty-one, I think that makes him a man. He's a soldier like you, Damien. Maybe you know him."

"Who the fuck—"

"I'm supposed to be meeting him at the movies, and I don't want to keep him waiting. So congratulations, and welcome to the family," Amira interrupted me, pulling Evita into a hug and she happily returned the gesture. When they pulled away, Amira peered over at me, placing her hand over my heart. "You should probably start on that baby-making thing. You are getting kind of old."

Everyone burst out laughing. Everyone but me.

"Anyway, congratulations, Damien. I'm sure you and Evita will be very happy. You have that effect on women," she snidely spoke, hugging and kissing Rosarío next. Telling her she wouldn't be home too late before leaving without so much as another glance my way.

I spent the rest of the evening with my blood boiling and my temper igniting. Neither of which were ever good when it came to Amira. I was a ticking fucking time bomb, about to explode with every second I had to sit there and pretend like I wasn't plotting the murder of her goddamn boyfriend.

By the time we said our goodbyes and I dropped Evita off at her house, it was well past eleven o'clock at night. I lied to my fiancée, telling her I had an early morning meeting and needed to take off. She understood, not paying me any mind. It wasn't the first time I couldn't spend the night because of Emilio.

I drove back to Rosarío's like a bat out of fucking hell; I couldn't get to Amira fast enough. I parked my car on the street in front of the house. Right when I stepped out of my car, I heard a slight echo of what sounded like a moan. It was coming from the direction of the small park a few houses down. Putting a halt to everything in my crazed mind, I made my way over there on pure compulsion. Realizing very fucking quickly that the sounds were coming from the backseat of a piece of shit car.

Call it instinct.

Perception.

Fucking madness.

I knew it was Amira who was underneath the motherfucker who was about to die.

Rage quickly took over every last fiber of my being. I took off, hauling ass toward the car like a possessed man. Needing to confirm my suspicions.

I growled, roughly swinging open the backdoor, barging in on the act. "What. The. Fuck!"

Amira screeched, “Damien!” Her dress was bunching at her waist, her bra straps were hanging down her arms, and one of her breasts was exposed. If she didn’t have any panties on, I was going to do much more damage than just having it out with her.

The piece of shit’s hand moved from in between her legs, turning to see who was behind him. I didn’t give him the chance. I gripped onto his hair, crudely yanking him backward out of the car. His hand immediately went toward my vicious hold, trying to pry me off.

“Damien, no!”

I didn’t waver, slamming him face first onto the trunk of his car. His body jolted as he stumbled around to face me.

“Fuck, man! I’m her boyfriend!” he reasoned.

“I don’t give of a fuck if you’re Jesus! You don’t fucking touch her!” I seethed. Using his momentum, my fist connected with his jaw before he even saw it coming.

His face snapped back, taking half his body with him. I was over to him in one stride, grabbing ahold of his collar and punching his fucking face repeatedly. Delivering a blow to his stomach, then his ribs. Hearing a hasty crack in my fist’s wake. Letting go, he fell to the ground, covered in blood and whimpering in pain.

“Damien, please stop this!” she shouted from the backseat, franticly trying to fix her dress to cover herself up. Only fueling my fury.

“Get up!” I snarled, kicking him repeatedly in the side. Making him recoil in more of the agony I was vivaciously delivering.

I ignored her pathetic pleas, continuing my assault on this motherfucker’s face and body. I hit him until my knuckles felt raw.

Amira flew out of the car, her dress still barely covering her. Her tit still out on display. “Oh my God, Damien, enough!”

I hovered above him, panting. My chest rising and falling, ready to let him up. He rolled over onto his back, and it was then I noticed his fucking belt and pants were undone.

Amira saw where my glare went, and she immediately argued, “It’s not what you think.”

I didn’t give her a chance to explain. I leaned forward, grabbed his belt buckle and whipped it out of the loops of his jeans, pulling it off of him. Her eyes immediately widened, knowing what I was about to do. I snapped the belt back and it whizzed in the air, landing right on his cock.

Knocking him the fuck out.

“Holy fuck,” she breathed out, instantly falling to her knees on the pavement to tend to him. I halted her attempt, clutching onto her wrists. Roughly yanking her to her feet, turning her to face me instead.

She didn’t back down, using all her strength to shove me away. “Who the hell do you think you are?! Don’t you have a fiancée you should be making babies with?”

“Enough!” I ordered, barely wavering from her futile attempts.

“Fuck you! I can’t believe you just did that! He’s my boyfriend! We weren’t doing anything that you’ve never done! In front of me! I hate you, Damien! I fucking hate you so much!” she seethed, tears falling down the sides of her face as she started to slam her fists into my chest.

I let her take her aggression out on me. I allowed her to scream, hit me, and do whatever the fuck she needed to calm her ass down. It was no secret in Rosarío’s neighborhood of who I was. Every last one of them feared Emilio, which meant they feared me. No one would dare call the police, knowing the consequences would end in death. The police were null and void. Emilio owned them.

“Why? Why do you keep doing this to me? What have I ever done to you, to make you treat me like this! I’m not your fucking doormat, Damien! Stop treating me like one!”

I immediately let her go, her words hitting me as hard as the beating that motherfucker on the ground just took. She stumbled, trying to catch her footing. Surprised I released her.

"Jesus Christ, Amira! I didn't protect you all these years so you could become a whore. Fucking random guys in the backseat of their cars!"

She cold-cocked me, punching me right in the jaw. Screaming out from the pain it caused her, "You bastard! I wasn't fucking him! We were just fooling around."

I cocked my head to the side, moving my jaw from side-to-side. "So you're pissed that I didn't let you get off?"

"Oh, don't worry about that. He gets me off plenty already."

I scoffed, "I bet your papi would be real proud of the whore you've become."

She stood taller, stepping up into my face. "I'd rather be his whore than yours, any day."

I jerked back, stunned by her bluntness. She didn't hesitate. "We're done here." Turning around once again, returning to the piece of trash. Choosing him over me.

"I never wanted you to find out I was engaged that way," I honestly spoke, needing her to finally hear my truths. Stopping her dead in her tracks. "I never wanted to hurt you, Muñeca."

Even though her back was to me, I knew she grimaced. I hadn't called her that in probably close to two years, when it was all I used to address her by. She took a deep breath before turning around to stare me deep in the eyes, stating, "All you've done over the last two years is hurt me, Damien."

"I know."

"Why? When you know you love me. I mean, look at him." She gestured to the son of a bitch on the ground. "You beat my boyfriend senseless because you can't stand the thought of another man in my life. Who does that? For over two years all, you've wanted is to push me away and make me move on. And when I finally do… you try to kill him. Where in your head does that even make sense? How do you even rationalize that? You're engaged! Do you know what that means? You're getting married. You're going to have a family, a future. A life. What am I supposed to do? Sit around and just watch? How selfish is that?"

"If I was truly selfish, Amira. I'd still be in your life."

She shook her head, scowling. "You can't have it both ways. Remember that little fact when you go home to your *luz*."

I pulled my hair back away from my face, wanting to tear it the fuck out. "What do you want me to say? Eh? That I love you? That I've always loved you? Is that what you need to hear?"

"No, Damien. Not anymore. You wanted me out of your life. Well, guess what? Now I want you out of mine. You've been telling me since day one that you're not the man I thought you were, and you're right. You're not. I don't know who you are, and I never did." She pointed to her boyfriend again. "This. This was my breaking point. You don't want me to be happy. All you want is for me to burn in the darkness with you. Well, I can't do that anymore."

"Do you think it's been easy for me to push you away? That I haven't wanted to make you *mine* when I know no matter what, you always will be. All I've ever wanted to do is protect you and keep you safe. Even if it cost me having you in my life."

She walked over, stopping a few inches from me. Placing her hand over my heart. "I'm safe, okay? You got what you wanted. I let you go. Please, Damien, now it's your turn to do the same."

I held my head up higher, maintaining my strong composure. Knowing it was what she needed. When all I wanted to do was fall apart.

To give me the last bit of *her*, she stood on the tips of toes, leaned in, and kissed my cheek. Whispering, "If she loves you half as much as I do, your life will be wonderful."

For the first time, I watched her turn her back on me and walk away. Conscious of the fact that this turn in events was what was needed for her to truly not be in my life.

She needed to leave me because I would've never been able to leave her.

And that was the reality of our love story.

19

Damien

I picked Evita up, carrying her over the threshold of our honeymoon suite.

"Damien! Put me down!" she laughed, loving every second of our sacred day.

We were married at six o'clock in the evening at the Cathedral of San Cristóbal, Havana. Where there couldn't have been more than twenty people in attendance. Emilio and Rosarío were of course, sitting front and center on the groom's side for the nuptials. My father was on guard with Pedro and a few others at the entrances, much to my disapproval. I didn't invite the fucking bastard. Amongst the guests were some acquaintances of mine from school that I made throughout almost six years. The bride's side included a few of Evita's friends and some other random patrons. The rest of the pews were occupied with colleagues of Emilio's, whom he insisted needed to be invited for negotiating tactics. How my wedding turned into a political debate was beyond me.

During the ceremony, my eyes kept shifting to the first pew. Waiting for the one person I truly wanted to see appear. Even though I knew she couldn't be there for obvious reasons, something told me she wouldn't have come even if she could have. I hadn't seen Amira since the last time she walked away from me, well over a year ago. I respected her request and officially let her go. Making sure I kept my distance at all costs, but continued to make sure she stayed off Emilio's radar. I still stopped by Rosarío's every once in a while, to catch up with her. Doing my best to avoid the times when Amira was around every time I showed up. I stopped asking about her after a few months, having no idea what she was up to, other than she still lived with Rosarío, and as far as I knew, she had no intentions of moving out. Even though it had been over half a year since she legally became an adult, turning eighteen.

She was never far from my mind, and I knew she never would be. One day while shopping, I couldn't fucking help myself, I bought her a doll for old time's sake with a card on her birthday that said, "This reminded me of better times. Happy birthday, Muñeca." She never replied, not that I expected her to.

I couldn't believe I was almost twenty-eight years old and married to a woman who'd become such a huge part of my life. I threw my new bride on the bed, hovering above her. She watched me with a greedy stare as I removed my suit jacket and loosened my tie. Throwing them both on the bed next to her. She grabbed the long piece of silk I had just removed, holding it out in front of her and arching an eyebrow. Her eyes followed the movement of my hands while I was unbuttoning my dress shirt, pulling it out from my slacks to wear it open. I placed my hands in my pockets, not ready to give her what she wanted.

At least, not until she begged for it.

"Who said that was yours?" I asked, grinning.

"I thought what yours is mine now. Isn't that the way marriage goes?"

"You mean, what's yours is mine and what's mine is *mine*. Including you."

She sat up on her knees, throwing my tie around my neck. "Does that mean you're not mine then?"

"I'm yours." I leaned forward, slowly running my lips against hers. Tempting her with my tongue.

"I love you, Damien."

"I know." Even after all this time it was still hard for me to tell her I loved her, but she knew it though.

She pecked my lips. "What do we do now?"

"You bring your ass over here." I kissed her.

"What's wrong with my ass?"

"It's not on my fucking cock."

She smiled wide against my lips. "Oh, it's going to be that kind of night."

"We both know how this night is going to end. With my tongue on your clit and your pussy sliding down my dick."

"Well, if that's the case, then let me slip into something a little more comfortable."

I suddenly shoved her backward onto the bed, crawling my way up her body. "Try to leave. I fucking dare you."

I spent the next few hours fucking my wife. Consummating our marriage on every surface in the suite. Making a mental note to leave the cleaning service a hefty tip for the cleanup. She was lucky I took mercy upon her, allowing her a break to go shower. I heard the water running, and I resisted the urge to go fuck her in there too. Instead, I went and grabbed our bags from my car, setting hers on the floor in the bathroom when I returned. She said some shit about wanting to slip into something she knew I would supposedly like.

I threw my bag on the bed, walked over to the mini-bar and poured myself a glass of bourbon and my bride a flute of champagne. After twenty minutes of waiting for Evita to emerge, I decided to get some work done. Grabbing the files Emilio gave me just after the ceremony and taking a seat at the table directly in front of the bathroom, I opened the documents one by one.

Each file put together a piece of a puzzle I never knew I was a part of. Completely understanding why Emilio was so insistent that I go over the folder as soon as possible. I had no fucking idea my wedding night would turn into this, but with that said, I didn't regret looking. Not for one fucking second. There was no way I could protect her from this, the images alone were enough to send me to my goddamn knees. Spinning the wheels in motion. Picture after picture of her small frame, her brown eyes, her beautiful smile. The way her hair was always cascading down her back, framing her gorgeous fucking face.

I shuffled through a few more photos, coming across the documents that I read closely. Rereading them over and over again in the little window of time I had. Forever memorizing each and every detail. Only confirming what the images already proved. Phone conversations translated onto paper, numbers, dates. One in particular standing out amongst the rest. It was all blatantly in front of me, clear as fucking day. There weren't any misconceptions or false accusations, the proof was fucking blinding me. There was no room for error or gray area.

It was all written out in black and white.

Fighting, battling, toying with my need to protect her and love her like I always had. For the first time since I met her all those years ago, it was now a raging war between…

She and I.

The sound of the bathroom door opening and Evita walking out brought my attention up to her. She looked like a fucking goddess, wearing a silk white matching bra and panty set with fuck me heels. I leaned back into my chair, setting my ankle over my knee. Taking in the vision in front of me, not believing my eyes. I made a twirling gesture with my fingers, and she understood my silent command. Smiling as she spun in a slow circle, showing me exactly what I wanted to see. Stopping once she was facing me again.

"Come here," I demanded, rubbing my lips in a back and forth motion with my index and middle fingers.

She did, making sure to sway her luscious ass with each step she took in my direction. I nodded toward the table in front of me for her to sit down and spread her fucking legs. She seductively licked her lips with nothing but hunger in her eyes for what was to come. Lifting herself up onto the cool wood surface, doing what I had ordered.

I eyed her up and down, taking in every last curve of her body, every last inch of silky white skin. Making her pussy clench from the predatory regard of my penetrating glare. There wasn't one nook of her figure that I didn't explore with my hands, my tongue, my lips, my fucking cock.

A nostalgic state of mind fell over me like I never felt before.

"You want to know what I thought when I first met you?" I questioned in a neutral tone, when I was feeling everything but that.

She beamed, nodding. Her expression consuming me as much as her beating heart.

"I thought you looked so goddamn innocent, and all I wanted to do was fuck you."

She mischievously smiled, leaning forward to touch me. Instantly stalling when she saw the gun in my hand, resting on my lap. Her eyebrows narrowed. "Why are you holding that?" she asked, barely above a whisper.

"So tell me, Evita. How innocent are you?"

"Damien, I—" I sharply sat forward, making her jolt back. Away from me.

"What's wrong, baby? You scared?" I rasped, placing my gun on her thigh, leisurely moving it up her leg toward her chest. Inch by inch, wanting her to feel the cool metal against her heated skin. I added, "You should be."

Her eyes widened and her nostrils flared, causing her face to pale. "I love you," she muttered, loud enough for me to hear. Her voice was trembling along with her pouty fuck-me lips.

"Is that right? How much do you love me, Evita? Tell me, baby? Enough to die for me? Or enough to kill for me?"

Her body shivered, creating goose bumps all over her skin. Looking back and forth between the gun that was now near her pussy and the man holding it.

Me.

She sucked in a breath, her mouth suddenly dry. "Why are you asking me this?"

I ignored her question, slowly continuing my calculated descent. Making sure to always have my steady finger over the trigger. Needing her to understand that I would always be the one in control. I purposely moved my gun back and forth over her breasts, letting the end of the barrel linger over her heart. Fucking with her emotions in the same way she fucked with my heart.

"Did you know who I was from the start?"

She shook her head, never taking her eyes off my gun. That was currently on top of her rapidly beating heart.

"No? Want to answer that again? Except this time, I advise you not to lie to my goddamn face."

"I'm not lying. Why would I know you?" she let out, blinking her eyes.

I briefly pulled away the gun. Her hand flew to her chest, and she visibly released the breath I knew she had been holding the second she saw my gun. "Damien, you had me terrified there for a second," she nervously laughed. "I'm all for role playing, just a little warning next time. Alright?"

Reaching under my leg, I chucked the files onto her lap. "Open them," I simply stated.

"Why?"

I abruptly stood, causing her to jump out of her skin. Her eyes were glued to every movement of my body as I carelessly waved my gun around in front of me. Letting her know this role playing was far from fucking over.

"Goddamn it, Evita! You know how much I hate to fucking repeat myself! Now pull your head out of your ass, quit acting like a dumb blonde bitch, and open the fucking folders."

Her hands trembled as she grabbed the first file, turning over the cover to look at the first page. If I thought her face was pale before, well now it was bright fucking white. One by one she took in the pictures, the documents, the evidence; she couldn't decide what to focus on more. Exactly how I had felt for what seemed like hours ago.

"No…" She fervently shook my head. "No…" Unable to form any coherent thoughts, she stumbled on all the words coming out of my lying, betraying mouth.

"Since you're my fucking wife and all, I'll give you one last chance before I let a fucking bullet do the talking for you. Did you know who I was from the start?"

"Please, Damien, let me explain. I love you!"

I slammed my fists at the sides of her body on the table, welcoming the sting. It was a nice change from the one in my heart. She screamed, shuddering in terror as I eerily loomed in front of her. My hands never leaving her sides.

"I won't ask again," I gritted through a clenched jaw near her ear.

She intensely nodded. Her body quivering so fucking bad it vibrated the whole table. Placing my gun on her cheek, I hissed, "Good girl."

"Damien, please don't do this… please…"

I cocked my head to the side, taking in her pathetic pleas. Softly moving my mouth against her cheek and toward her lips, craving the feel of them against mine. "Did you think I wouldn't have found out?" I breathed into her mouth.

"I… please…"

"Choose your words wisely, Evita. I already know you're a fucking liar."

Tears streamed down her beautiful face. I didn't care. I didn't care about anything. I was too busy dying inside from the blade she stabbed in my heart.

"Please… just let me explain… I didn't…" She couldn't catch her breath as if the room started to spin on her.

Over.

And over.

And over.

“I swear, I love you.”

“I loved you, too, baby.”

She winced, hating to hear those words come out of my mouth. Knowing I meant them, but never said them.

“Do you have any idea what it feels like to have your heart ripped out? Because you will in a fucking second if you don’t answer my goddamn question!” I roared along her lips, aiming my gun toward her heart.

“No! Yes! No! I don’t know! I hoped… I prayed you wouldn’t have found out!” Her lips vibrated against mine, and I resisted the urge to bite them between my teeth.

“It always amazes me to see how fast people can shatter, and trust me when I say, baby, I’m about to fucking break you.”

More tears slid down her face, placing her hand over her stomach. Really wanting to hold it over her heart.

“How does it feel to know your life is about to end by the man you were supposed to kill?”

She shook her head back and forth. “No, no, no, no, no,” she repeated, looking me dead in the eyes. “I was never going to kill you. I swear it!”

“To know that the woman I made my wife is nothing but a fucking traitor? Now, that…” I kissed her. “That I didn’t see coming.”

“I’m sorry… I’m so sorry… but I love you! I didn’t know I was going to fall in love with you! I was just supposed to be a mole in your life for a few months! The U.S. wanted to take down Emilio, not you! But they knew that you were the way to him! They promised me they would send me to America in exchange for any information I could provide! I just wanted to get the fuck out of Cuba! This bullshit communist country that took my parents' lives!"

"So was anything you told me the truth? Or was it all a bunch of bullshit lies? Starting with your 'I love you's'."

"I was never going to kill you! I promise!"

"Your promises mean shit to me. Exactly the same way you now do."

She shut her eyes, she had to. The pain of my words taking her under.

"I thought I met the woman I was going to spend the rest of my life with. You. Someone who understood me, never judged me. It all makes sense now. How you always wanted to know about my day, that it never mattered the lives I took, the sins I'd pay. All you wanted was information on Emilio, that's why you stood the fuck by my side, no matter what. I let you in, Evita. In my life. My home. My bed. My fucking heart!" I snarled, unable to go on with this charade of blatant treachery any longer. Shoving the end of my gun harder into her heart. "You're nothing but a lying cunt!"

"Damien, please… I'm begging you… please…"

I kissed her one last time, needing to remember her just this way before backing away, keeping the aim of my gun over her heart. I ordered, "Get on your fucking knees."

She didn't. Her body was shaking profusely, unable to breathe.

To think.

To move.

"NOW!"

Placing her hands in the air out in front of her, as if that was going to make one bit of difference. She listened, sliding to the ground onto her knees in front of me.

"You can't judge a sinner by one sin alone, and I've sinned enough to reap what I sow. You know what I do to people who betray me, fucking traitors… it's who I am. It's all I know," I firmly stated, tears forming in my eyes. “For better or for worse, right, baby?”

Evita. Knew. Me.

She should’ve known better.

“Damien, I lov—” I cocked my gun back, and her eyes widened in panic, fear, understanding.

“You know, I always preferred the till death do us part.”

And with that… I didn’t hesitate in pulling the trigger. Ending the life of another fucking traitor, except the only difference was…

This one *was* my wife.

20 Damien

I drove my car down the winding roads in a vacant state. My body was stiff, my face showed no emotion, and I felt absolutely fucking nothing. I'd been like this for the last six months, moving on autopilot. I couldn't remember the last time I slept for more than an hour or two. My mind wouldn't stop reeling, playing out my entire fucking life every time I closed my eyes.

It was a whirlwind of emotions.

A catalyst of memories.

An unrelenting nightmare I was living in broad daylight.

Despite my numb state, I was still able to graduate at the top of my class and early from law school. It was the only thing that kept me going. I drowned myself in school work, classes, and Emilio. Going as far as picking up some extra shifts at the prison to take out my frustrations through torturous acts. Dreadfully trying to get through the days and nights. Knowing nothing would change. Tomorrow would be the same as the day before. They were all on constant repeat, even though I was going forward in time. I tried not to think about Evita, mindful that everything she had ever told me was yet another fucking lie. I couldn't stand seeing, feeling, or smelling her presence around my apartment. I took care of the issue the only way I saw fit. I fucking burned her belongings.

The one woman I actually allowed into my real life, ended up being like the rest of them.

Another goddamn traitor.

Maybe it was my karma for all the lives I'd taken and the one heart I'd broken. Over and over again. Rosarío and Emilio were the only two people who knew the truth about Evita's untimely demise. There was no getting around the truth; it was what it was.

No fucking regrets.

I did what I had to do.

As always, Rosarío provided the support I needed, being the only mother I'd ever known. Emilio, on the other hand, patted my back and laughed it off. Saying some shit about all women being lying whores.

Amira tried to reach out to me after Evita's death a few times. I assumed Rosarío told her one thing or another, but never the truth. She left me countless messages that went unreturned but not unheard. I'd often sit out on the balcony and replay them just to hear her sweet voice that always brought me comfort in her absence and in my time of need. I tried like hell to not go to her. The last thing I wanted was for Amira to think she was my rebound. She didn't deserve all this fucked-up shit, she never asked for it. She certainly wouldn't give a shit about the fucking birthday present I was about to deliver.

But *I* did.

As much as I wished I didn't, I cared. A lot. I had missed her last few birthdays, and it almost crushed me not being there for all her important days. I spent her last birthday with Evita in my bed and Amira on my mind. I wasn't about to miss this one too. I just needed to see her face, wish her a happy birthday, and talk to her for a few minutes, if she would allow it. Those were my only intentions and expectations as I drove over to Rosarío's house, feeling a sense of something I couldn't even explain or begin to understand.

Maybe it was the feeling of going home.

Then again, it could have just been Amira. The only person on the entire planet that could physically bring me to my fucking knees with as little as a look.

I didn't deserve her.

I never asked for her.

I couldn't have been more grateful to have her.

Amira didn't deserve me either, but no amount of training could ever condition her out of my life. I'd conformed to a lot of things I wasn't proud of, but Amira would never be one of them. She had always been my refuge from the chaos going on in my daily life.

She was the exception.

She was *my* exception.

Deep down I was hoping she wouldn't be home, but even deeper than that, I prayed she was. My heart sped up a few extra beats when I stepped out of my car. Once again, I thought about how unprepared I was to actually see her. It felt like a lifetime had passed since we had talked, over a year and a half ago. This was the longest span of time I'd ever gone without her. My adrenaline pumped wildly through my veins with each step that brought me closer to the entrance.

To her.

With a long, deep, reassuring breath, I walked up the stairs to the porch and just as I was about to knock, the light flicked on and the door opened. I wasn't expecting to come face to face with Amira. Her expression left me in a state of fucking shock, not really knowing what to say or how to even say it.

For a brief second, we both stood there without saying a word. I spent the last six months dead inside, and all it took was one fucking moment between us to feel alive again.

She was so fucking perfect.

So fucking mine.

She was wearing a pair of pink cotton shorts and a tight white tank top. Without even dropping my eyes, I could see her midriff where her tank didn't quite cover her sun-kissed skin. She held a bowl in her hands with strawberry ice cream melting inside. She'd always stir it in a circle until it was a smooth and creamy consistency before she'd eat it. It was one of her silly quirks I'd grown to love. I tried to focus on anything other than the deafening silence between us, keeping me from forming any coherent thoughts. Not one single word came to my mind. When I had thousands I wanted to say to her.

She was the first to break the silence, saying, "She's not home. Mama Rosa went to Havana to help a friend. Something you would know nothing about. I'll tell her you stopped by." Her trying to slam the fucking door in my face was the only trigger I needed to snap out of my hypnotic state. The best thing about my personality was my ability to act quickly, and this was my moment to strike.

My hand stopped the door faster than she could close it, and I easily held her and the solid wood back. "I didn't come to see her. Let me in, open the door," I ordered in a neutral, but demanding, tone.

"Why? What do you want, Damien?"

"You know what I want. It's your birthday."

"Yeah? I had one last year too, and the year before that and the year before that, and you didn't bother to show up for any of those either."

"I stopped by for your seventeenth birthday, and you weren't here. I had a gift delivered for your eighteenth birthday, but it went unacknowledged, by you. Now I'm standing here for your nineteenth birthday with yet another gift, so please open the goddamn door."

"What happened on my sixteenth birthday, Damien? Huh? Oh, yeah! I remember, you fucked a woman in front of me! Now, guess what? I don't want anything from you other than for you to leave!"

Without a fight, I pushed through the door, moving her out of the way so I could gaze into her solemn eyes. "You know you don't mean that. I fucked up, Amira. All I do is fuck up when it comes to you. But I still remember the girl who used to anxiously wait for me in her reading nook that I built just for her. You love gifts. You always have. It's why you look forward to your birthday and Christmas, and all the times you knew I was coming to see you. I did nothing but fucking spoil you, and now all I want to do is to give you my gift. If you still want me to leave after you open it, I will. But I'm hoping that won't be the case."

She glanced at the package, wrapped in white paper with a satin blue bow in my arms and reluctantly nodded, letting me in. Probably because she knew I wouldn't leave until I got my way. My hand immediately touched her soft skin on the small of her back, causing her breath to hitch. She wasn't expecting to feel the emotions that the slightest bit of my touch could evoke. I hid back a smile, guiding her toward the couch in the living room to sit down, internally struggling to let her go.

"Damien, I don't know if this is such—"

I grabbed the bowl out of her lap, quickly replacing it with my present. Trying to distract her from what she was going to say. "Pull the ribbon," I insisted, crouching down in front of her to explain as she opened it.

Amira did as she was told, pulling off the bow and lifting the lid from the package. I couldn't fucking resist, I never could when it came to her, and I took a bite of her ice cream. Knowing her sweet mouth was on the exact same spoon minutes ago.

The expression on her face pulled me away from my conscious thoughts, assuring me that she had no idea what the gift was. She took out the handcrafted box and held it out in front of her. "I don't get it. What's it supposed to be?"

Taking one last bite of ice cream, I traded her the bowl for the box. Lifting the silver lid, showing her exactly how it worked. "A guy in Havana makes them. It's made from clay and when you put a candle in it, it heats up to help keep you warm."

She sucked in her bottom lip, stirring her ice cream. Trying to act unfazed like she wasn't the least bit interested, but I knew she was. "So what's so special about that?"

I was unable to hold back a smile that time, her snarky little mouth always had a way of making me laugh. I reached for the candle that was still inside the wrapping and set the box on the end table next to us. Quickly turning off the lamp, needing the room to be somewhat dark in order for her gift to work.

"The special part comes when you light the candle and place the lid back on top of the box," I told her, handing her the wooden matches out of my pocket. "Go ahead, light the candle, Muñeca."

I hadn't called her that in years, and it felt so fucking perfect falling from my lips. For a few more seconds, her eyes stayed connected to mine and it was clear that she was thinking the same thing I was. But she shook it off, continuing to act unfazed like the term of endearment didn't mean anything to her, when it meant everything to the both of us. She lit the matchstick and leaned forward to light the candle.

"Look up, Amira."

Her eyes noticeably widened, and her mouth dropped open when her eyes gazed up at me. I swear I heard a gasp escape her lips as she took in the significance and sentiment behind her gift. She opened her mouth several times to say something, though nothing came out. She couldn't speak. She could barely even keep up with all the memories tumbling down on her from that night. I took it upon myself to speak for her, pointing to the stars on the ceiling, and connecting the dots in the same way she had in the night sky, four years ago.

Repeating her same words, I reiterated, "That's Princess Andromeda and that's her husband, Perseus. Do you see how they unite in the middle? You can't tell where one star ends and the other begins, kind of like they're holding hands."

For a few moments, I had all of her…

Her mind.

Her body.

Her soul.

Her heart.

They all came back to me, like they had never left to begin with.

They've always been mine.

"Wow… Damien, I can't… I mean… wow…" she breathed out, running her hand over the warming box. "What are these stars?" she questioned in an engrossed tone, gliding the tips of her fingers over the blue stars and then the only silver one.

"Nine kids," I said, light-heartedly with a grin, hoping for a smile.

I got a condescending glare, instead. "Why is there only one silver?"

"The blue ones are all boys."

And there it was. The giggle that got me through so much fucking shit. To this day it was the sweetest sound I'd ever heard. I had almost forgotten what it sounded like, and that was something I never wanted to forget. Even if it was quickly silenced, it was enough to take me a long, long, fucking way.

"Thank you, Damien, but none of this changes anything. You can't show up here after a year and a half with a present and think everything is okay. It's not. I tried calling you, I stopped by your apartment even though I promised myself I'd never step foot in there again. But I did it for you. I was worried about you. I mean, I can't imagine what it was like to lose your wife. To a car accident of all things."

I kept my composure, knowing it was the lie that Rosarío conjured up to tell her. Simply stating, "We're not talking about her."

"I know… I get it… To love someone and—"

"I love *you*, Muñeca. I've always loved you, and I always will." It was the first time I'd ever expressed those three words to her out loud. I had to finally say them. They stayed dormant, pent up in me for as long as she had been in my life. She didn't try to hide the heartwarming expression on her face this time. Even though she already knew my feelings, I think a part of her also knew how hard it was for me to express them to her.

To anyone…

But especially *her*.

She swallowed hard. "Damien—"

I was over to her in one stride, sitting on the coffee table in front of her. I placed my hands on the sides of her face and gazed deep into her eyes underneath our stars. Finally uttering my fucking truth to her. "I came here to wish you a happy birthday, to give you your gift, and to tell you I fucking love you, Muñeca. I will always, no matter what, love you. I need you to remember that. You think you could do that for me?"

Her eyes followed my every word. They were my undoing, filled with so much love for me still, but in one quick movement, she grabbed my wrists, pulled my hands off the sides of her face, and stood. Walking away, leaving me sitting there wondering what the fuck just happened.

With a cold stare, she instantly spewed, "Who the fuck do you think you are? You think you can just show up here one day and…and what, Damien? Pick up where we left off?" She glared at me, slowly shaking her head in a calculated motion. "Like we're just going to go back to the time you looked at me like someone you used to know? Or worse, someone you didn't?"

I stood, abruptly walking over to her. She didn't cower down when my large, muscular frame overshadowed hers as I pressed her against the wall. Closing her in with my arms at the sides of her face, needing to prove my fucking point. Her resolve shattered when I leaned forward, slowly moving my lips over to her ear. My hot breath igniting tingles to run down her spine. I whispered, "I miss you. I love you. I'm in love with you." One by one her reactions radiated off her skin, causing all sorts of other sensations. I had my girl right where I wanted her.

Vulnerable.

I could feel her tense frame tremble at my mercy. Knowing damn well I was at her mercy too.

It didn't take much for my mouth to near hers. I pulled her closer to me by the nook of her neck until I could feel her unstable breath against my lips. Assaulting every last fiber of my fucking being.

I groaned inches away from her lips, "Does this feel like someone who doesn't know you?"

"You can't—"

"I can't do what? Eh? Tell me, Muñeca? What the fuck can't I do? Because I'm not the one who's pretending like they don't know every last thing about me." I suddenly grabbed her wrists and brought them above her head. Holding them hostage in my tight grasp while I softly gripped onto the front of her neck. My thumb and index finger clutched over her pulse that heightened with my touch. "All I've ever done is try to protect you. From Emilio, from my father… from *me*."

She shut her eyes, my words too painful for her to hear.

"You're safe, and that's all that has ever mattered to me. You deserve so much more than anything I could ever offer you, Amira. But exactly like those constellations, neither one of us knows where one starts or the other ends. And nothing will ever fucking change that," I vowed close to her lips.

I wanted to touch her.

I wanted to kiss her.

Mostly, I wanted to fucking claim her.

Never understanding how something so wrong…

Could feel so fucking right.

I was the first to pull away from her. If I didn't, I wouldn't have been able to let her go. I accomplished what I came for, and it was time for me to leave. She immediately opened her eyes, staring intently into mine as if she knew what I was thinking. Not wanting me to go as much as I didn't want to fucking leave.

"I'm sorry, Muñeca. For the past, for now, for the future… for everything." With that I kissed the top of her head, letting my lips linger for a few seconds too long before I reluctantly let her go. Walking toward the front door, leaving everything I ever wanted behind.

Her.

21

Amira

I placed his gift on my nightstand, gazing up at the stars on my ceiling for I don't know how long, when I finally pulled myself away to go shower. I was more confused now by his unexpected visit than I was before he even showed up on my doorstep. His sudden presence opened up old wounds, and I felt like I was breaking all over again. I had come to accept what had happened between us, but I had never forgotten. I was healing until he showed up, painfully ripping the Band-Aid from my already sensitive skin. Taking any progress I had made, away. That was the thing about Damien, he was a paradox of contradictions. His words always spoke one thing, but his actions always proved another.

I stayed under the warm running water, reflecting on everything from the night, until the spray turned cold. Grabbing a towel, I wrapped it around my wet body and made my way back to my bedroom. Just wanting to pass the hell out and avoid any more conflicting emotions he seemed to always stir inside of me.

For the first time in years, I walked into the room we once shared with nothing but the constellations from the candle lighting up the room. Stopping just outside the door to take in the shadowy figure roaming freely.

Damien was there, when I had just watched him leave. He was standing in the middle of the room, looking around the space. Observing how nothing in my room had changed, even though so much between us had.

"I couldn't get rid of them," I announced from the doorway behind him, watching as he took in all the gifts he'd given me throughout the years. "I tried. Several times. So many times, I've lost count. Whenever I pulled something off one of the shelves, it just felt wrong. Like I was throwing you away, and as much as I wanted to get rid of you, Damien, I couldn't. You see, I want to hate you. I want to hate you so much, but I can't. I can't because I love you too fucking much. Do you have any idea how that feels? To love a man who can't… won't… love you back."

He slowly turned around, knowing precisely how he'd find me.

Naked.

Wet.

In nothing but a towel.

In two strides, he closed the distance between us with so much force I slammed against the wall behind me. Hitting it with a hard thud. He instantly caged me in with his arms, making me feel his love and his hate.

Not for me.

For himself.

"What are you doing, Damien?" I breathlessly asked, licking my lips like I was preparing them for him.

"I have no fucking idea, Muñeca," he admitted, once again leaning in close to my mouth. "I never do with you." He softly pecked my lips, waiting for my reaction.

I moaned, giving him exactly what he wanted.

And it was all he needed to lose control.

He roughly gripped onto my waist, lifting me up for my thighs to straddle his waist. Pulling me close to his body.

His chest.

His heart.

He kissed me, parting my lips with his tongue as he carried me over to the bed. The same mattress I'd slept next to him on so many times in the past. When he'd soothe my nightmares, chasing away the monsters from my sleep as much as he did the ones when I was awake. He gently laid me down, spreading my legs to lay in between them, lowering himself onto my heated body. Cradling my face, he never once broke our kiss.

Our connection.

Our love for one another.

There was something different about him as he hovered above me in a way I'd never experienced with him before. Like he was trying to show me a side to him that he didn't even know existed. Tenderly, he kissed me deep as his hands gently ran down my shoulders to pull the towel off my body.

"Damien," I nervously rasped, trembling beneath him, and he was barely even touching me.

I had no idea what I was in for.

"Shhh… it's me, Muñeca. It's me. I'm here, shhh..." he murmured, the same words he'd always used to calm me. Except, this was for entirely different reasons.

It worked enough to ease my worry. I visibly relaxed back into the sheets as he completely removed both the towel and himself off my body. I inadvertently whimpered, not only from the loss of his touch, but also from what I knew he desperately wanted to see. I could feel his eyes looking at every last inch of my skin for the first time ever, and I couldn't help but feeling insecure. I didn't have Evita's voluptuous body. I swear I sensed his stare roaming over my perky breasts, to my tan nipples, down to my narrow, slim waist. Slowly, deliberately, taking his time. My thighs clenched together when I felt his stare heading toward my most sacred area.

He lightly grabbed onto my knees, gradually spreading my legs open for him. Further and further apart. "It's me, Muñeca. I need to see what's always been fucking mine."

My face turned another shade of red in both desire and embarrassment, from being spread wide open for him. I could feel my wetness pooling in between my legs from his words and touch. Fueling my need to feel him, anywhere and everywhere. He caused another whimper to escape my lips when I felt his hand slowly expose my clit.

"Amira," he huskily groaned in a voice I'd never heard before. "Open your eyes. I need you to look at me while I'm looking at you."

I released the breath I didn't realize I was holding and locked eyes with his hooded stare.

They were foreign.

Unfamiliar.

And everything I ever wanted.

"Damien, I'm—"

"I've never wanted anything as much as I want you, Muñeca."

I didn't know how far this was going to go, but I didn't hesitate in breathing out, "Then take me."

He didn't have to be told twice. Removing his jacket, he threw it on the floor beside my towel. As he laid down on his stomach, he held onto my thighs and buried his face in between my legs.

My eyes widened. "What are you—"

"Shhh," he hummed, sucking my clit into his mouth.

My back jolted off the bed, making him chuckle as he moved his head up and down, side-to-side, using his tongue to vibrate against my core. "Mmmm… Damien," I purred, grabbing ahold of his hair as he continued with his oral assault. He never stopped working me over with his lips and tongue when he started to slide his finger into my soaking wet welcoming heat.

"Oh, God…" I moaned, curving my back into the mattress beneath me. Entirely coming undone from his touch.

He devoured me with his tongue and fingers, making love to me with his mouth. Sucking harder and more demanding with each passing second, to the point I thought I was going to pass the hell out. I knew he'd done this with women before, but it felt like he was experiencing the same new sensations I was. His mouth and hand were controlling my body, but my reactions were controlling his willpower to stay in control.

"Jesus… Damien… I can't… it's too much…"

A loud, rumbling growl escaped from deep within his chest. My words only proved all my thoughts right. He was losing control, and it was what made me completely surrender to the power he held over me.

I came.

I came so damn hard I saw stars. He didn't let up, making me come over and over again, against his fingers and mouth. I started to convulse, my body moving on its own accord. He instantly locked his arm around my lower torso, holding me in place. My back arched off the bed, my hands white-knuckled the sheets, and my body shook with so much force that I thought I would never stop coming undone.

"Oh, God… ahhh…" I profusely panted, my body turning on me.

Orgasm after orgasm. They were coming quick and fast, one right after the other with no end in sight. At least, not while he was in between my fucking legs.

"Please… Damien… please…" I squirmed, begging him to stop, tugging hard at his hair to the point I thought I was going to rip it out.

He released my clit with an unrelenting groan, not wanting to stop, but allowing me mercy. Thrusting his tongue into my heat, licking, eating, swallowing all my juices like I was his favorite meal. He slowly sat up with a pleased and satisfied expression on his face. Grinning as he shamelessly wiped his lips and chin with the back of his arm. Showing me precisely how much I came only because of him.

"That's all you, Muñeca. Your sweet pussy fucking squirted all over me."

His filthy words had as much effect on my body as his touch just did. I wanted him to say more dirty things like that to me. I never wanted it to end. He tore his shirt off by pulling it up from the back and over his head, throwing it on the floor beside the rest of our stuff as he started to unbuckle his belt and jeans. "Are you sure you want to do this? Just say the word, Amira, and I will stop now. Because I can guaran-fucking-tee that once I start, I won't be able to quit. Not with you. Not ever with fucking you."

I didn't falter, not for one second. "You promise?"

He smiled, sliding down his jeans, letting his hard cock jut free. My face paled, and my head jerked back against the pillow. "Damien… oh my God. You really are a monster."

He laughed so hard, throwing his head back.

"We can't. It won't fit. You'll kill me with that thing."

He mischievously grinned, crawling his way up my body, kissing and sucking his way up to my lips.

"I'm being serious, Damien. That thing is too big. It's too thick. I can't—"

He kissed me hard, stifling my words. "It's my cock, Muñeca." He kissed along my neck, down to the cleavage of my breasts. "Not my thing. My cock," he reaffirmed, peering up at me through the slits of his eyes. Simply stating, "Amira, you were made for me."

I beamed, understanding exactly what he was trying to say. He made his way back up to my lips, wanting to claim them again. Grabbing the hair by the nook of my neck, he brought my lips up to meet his, pecking me at first. Teasing them with the tip of his tongue, outlining my pouty mouth. My tongue sought his out, and our kiss quickly turned passionate, moving on its own accord. Taking what the other needed and vice versa.

He kissed me with everything he could muster up. He kissed me until the earth stopped moving and time stood still. There was something agonizing about the way we were moving—it was urgent, demanding, and all-consuming. We couldn't get enough of each other's taste, leaving us thirsty and wanting so much more.

I wanted everything.

He caressed the side of my face, my breasts, the back of my thighs as if he didn't know where he wanted to touch me the most.

"I love you, Muñeca," he throatily said in between our passionate kisses.

"I love you too," I panted, needing him to hear it as well.

He kissed me like his life depended on it. Like I was everything he ever wanted and so much more. I yearned for him to make us one person in the same way I always had before.

"Damien…" I moaned in a voice I didn't recognize.

Our bodies moved in sync like they were made for each other, nothing could ever compare or even come close to this. I placed my hand on his rapidly beating heart that was pounding against my chest and opened my eyes, staring profusely into his.

The devotion.

The adoration.

The love…

He had for me, spilled out of his dark, dilated, intensely piercing eyes.

"There she is… there's my girl," he rasped, slowly thrusting in.

"Ahhh… Damien..."

"Shhh… Muñeca, I got you."

I swear I felt every last inch of him as he tore his way through my virginity. My teeth bit into my bottom lip hard enough to taste blood. I probably should've told him I was still a virgin, though I was scared he would stop.

Or worse, he wouldn't do it all.

He slowly, tenderly thrust in and out of me, trying to steady his breathing, while I tried hard not to jerk away from him. I waited for the initial pain to subside, hoping like hell it didn't burn like this the entire time. My moans and whimpers weren't from pleasure, and it was then he knew.

He stopped, staring lovingly into my eyes. Contemplating what to say before he just whispered, "I'm so fucking in love with you, Muñeca..."

Emotions I'd never felt before flowed through my entire body while throbbing sensations took over the ache, relaxing my body a little more. Not only did Damien make slow, passionate love to me, he claimed me without words. His hips thrust harder and deeper into me with a compassionate, deliberate motion. I couldn't do anything but surrender to him. Submit to the only man I ever loved with my heart, body, and soul.

With every kiss, every touch, every thrust, and every single *I love you*, he made unspoken promises to me. He adoringly kissed all over my face, along my jawline, my forehead, and on the tip of my nose. The room started spinning like it did when his face was in between my legs. My head fell back, and my breathing became heady, urgent, and so good…

He immediately lapped at my neck and breasts, leaving tiny marks all over. I didn't want to move, I wanted to enjoy the sensation of him being on top of me.

"That feel good, baby?" he groaned, making his way back up to my mouth.

I nodded, unable to form words. My arms reached around him, hugging him closer against my body, wanting to feel his entire weight on me. He leaned his forehead on mine. Breathing out, "Open your eyes. Let me see those brown eyes, Muñeca."

I did, taking in how lively, thriving, and full of love his stare reflected back into mine. Our mouths were parted, still touching and panting profusely, trying to feel each and every sensation of our skin-on-skin contact. I swear the pounding of our hearts echoed off the walls.

"Fuck, baby… Come… come on my cock… just like that…"

Still no words.

I was coming. I was coming from my head to my toes, and all he needed was to keep doing whatever he was doing. A faint whimper turned into a moan when he angled my leg up higher, hitting that spot that his fingers did before. Like he could feel my silent pleas, he gave my throbbing nub some much-needed attention.

"You like that, Muñeca?" he questioned with warm words and passionate kisses to my lips.

"Damien…" I panted.

"Fuck, Amira… Fuck… you feel so good… so fucking tight… so fucking mine…" he growled, somewhere in between pleasure and pain.

I fell.

He fell.

We met somewhere in the middle. My entire world spun out of control, and so did his as I shuddered beneath him, and his body tensed above mine.

He was the beginning to my end or maybe it was the end to my beginning.

It didn't matter because he was my home too.

He would always be home to me.

"I love you, Damien."

Lifting his head, he kissed me. "You're the best thing that has ever happened to me. You know that, right?"

"Yes…" I smiled, returning his love. Nothing existed in that moment but him and me. No one else mattered, and my whole world was right here.

Right in this room.

I loved him.

I'd always loved him. And there was no doubt in my mind that Damien felt the same way.

This was the beginning.

Our beginning, and nothing or nobody could ever take it away. Not after tonight. He made love to me countless times, unable to satiate himself with my body. Until he let me fall asleep in his arms, in his world. As if I was his whole life, too. He held me so tight like he never wanted to let me go. At some point in the darkness, I felt him thrust back inside me. I was exhausted and sore, but it still felt so right. It almost felt like I was in and out of a dream. Except this time his love making felt different.

More vulnerable.

More powerless.

More urgent and frantic.

"Damien," I murmured, trying to open my eyes.

"Shhh… Muñeca… I'm here… Shhh… I'm here…"

Those words always soothed me, no matter if I was awake or asleep.

"I love you… I fucking love you…" he added in a desperate, desolate plea that I would remember for the rest of my life.

The next thing I knew I startled awake the following morning. Something woke me from a dead sleep. The front door maybe. I rolled over, letting it all sink in.

As soon as I saw her, I knew.

To the depths of my soul, I knew.

Yuly.

With a card that read, "Happy Birthday, Muñeca. I've never been your hero, but you have always been mine."

My heart exploded.

I died right then and there.

He wasn't trying to start a future with me. What I thought was our beginning was actually our end.

Our night.

The night, he spent hours worshipping me was his way of saying…

Goodbye.

Forever.

22
Damien

I've told you from the beginning of my story that I was nothing but a fucking monster.

At least now, you can't call me a liar…

to be continued...

EL PECADOR (The Sinner) book 2 and the conclusion of Damien and Amira's story will be releasing early January. El Pecador will be "Present time" and pre-order will be up very soon!

A note from the author:

Here you are, you made it to the end of book one. I'm sure you're probably cussing me out and scrolling through the pages to see if there is more. Allow me to explain; as much as I wanted to avoid El Santo ending on a cliffhanger, I couldn't. I actually have several chapters written from this point forward, which is in present time. The story was almost done, but as I was writing it, something felt off. I was rushing through present time to avoid having to make El Santo two books. To be completely honest, present time was what I was looking forward to writing the most and I was cutting so much out to make it one book. It wasn't fair for the storyline or to my characters and the story they wanted to tell. I decided pretty much at the last minute that I needed to stay true to my writing, the storyline, and characters by writing the best possible book so I decided it was best to make El Santo two books. I promise I'm not making you wait long, Part 2 which is "Present time" will be releasing early January with so much more story to tell. LOTS more angst, action, and of course love.

Thank you all so much for the continued love and support you always give me!! I couldn't do this without my bloggers and readers!!

I love you all so much!! <3

Connect with M

WEBSITE

FACEBOOK

INSTAGRAM

TWITTER

AMAZON PAGE

VIP READER GROUP

NEWSLETTER

EMAIL ADDRESS

El SANTO

MORE BOOKS BY M

All FREE WITH KINDLE UNLIMITED

EROTIC ROMANCE

VIP (The VIP Trilogy Book One)

THE MADAM (The VIP Trilogy Book Two)

MVP (The VIP Trilogy Book Three)

TEMPTING BAD (The VIP Spin-Off)

TWO SIDES GIANNA (Standalone)

CONTEMPORARY/NEW ADULT

THE GOOD OL' BOYS STANDALONE SERIES

COMPLICATE ME

FORBID ME

UNDO ME

El SANTO

CRAVE ME

EL DIABLO (THE DEVIL)

ROAD TO NOWHERE

ENDS HERE

54045208R00126

Made in the USA
Middletown, DE
02 December 2017